THE VIRGIN'S TEACHER

AN OLDER MAN YOUNGER WOMAN ROMANCE

ALISHA STAR

HOT AND STEAMY ROMANCE

CONTENTS

Blurb   v

1. Chapter One   1
2. Chapter Two   5
3. Chapter Three   13
4. Chapter Four   17
5. Chapter Five   25
6. Chapter Six   30
7. Chapter Seven   38
8. Chapter Eight   51
9. Chapter Nine   62
10. Chapter Ten   68
11. Chapter Eleven   88
12. Chapter Twelve   93
13. Chapter Thirteen   98
14. Chapter Fourteen   107
15. Chapter Fifteen   118
16. Chapter Sixteen   124
17. Chapter Seventeen   128
18. Chapter Eighteen   132

Sign Up to Receive Free Books   135
Preview of The Biker's Girl   137
Chapter One   139
Chapter Two   146

Other Books By This Author   155
Copyright   157

Made in "The United States" by:

Alisha Star

© Copyright 2020 – Alisha Star

ISBN: 978-1-64808-056-2

ALL RIGHTS RESERVED. No part of this publication may be reproduced or transmitted in any form whatsoever, electronic, or mechanical, including photocopying, recording, or by any informational storage or retrieval system without express written, dated and signed permission from the author

❀ Created with Vellum

BLURB

The Virgin's Teacher

His kid is amazing. He gets it from his dad, obviously. And I'm falling dangerously fast for my professor ...

I wasn't looking for anything but a little escape that night, okay? Not even looking for that, really, but my roommate Annie dragged me out to prevent me from combusting into nunhood. How was I supposed to know he'd be on the dance floor? What were the chances that the next day the same Adonis would walk into the class I'd just signed up for?
Not a good idea, Hannah.
But there was no escaping the attraction. My common sense ... just ... *poof.*
And then he asked me to babysit his kid.
Like I was going to say no to an adorable 7-year-old. Or to the chance to spend time with his dad.
Yes, I know; bad idea all around.
We agreed we were going to keep it totally professional.
That was doable, right?

WRONG.

'Doable' was Austin Parks, along with kind, funny, a great dad, an amazing teacher ...

So how did Mr. Amazing end up breaking my heart into a million smithereens? And can I ever forgive him?

A 7-year-old who needs a babysitter. A 20-something-year-old who set me on fire on the dance floor. And one major problem, namely, when she walked into my classroom the next day ...

What do you do when the first woman to light you up in years turns out to be your student?

Stay as far away as you can, obviously.

But what if she's as amazing as she is beautiful and she's willing to help out with your babysitting situation?

I can totally hire her and keep it on the level.

Just don't get me alone with her, ever ...

We're both adults. Yeah, there's an attraction between us. A major attraction. A flaming elephant in the room that can't be avoided. Except it has to be, right?

Well, matter of fact ...

WRONG!

There is no way I'm letting this one get away. She's the best thing to ever happen to me or my kid. Except that I'm sort of kind of ...

A total jerk.

Yeah, I own it. Can I ever win her back after my colossal screw up, though? I have to. Because my life isn't worth anything without Hannah Cosgrove in it.

CHAPTER ONE

"You need to get out and par-tay!" Annie yelled into my face, breathing her cranberry vodka breath all over me. I rolled my eyes. I always tried to be the voice of reason, but somehow Annie always got her way.

"I need to get some sleep, is what I need," I replied tartly. "I've got an intense semester ahead. Who knows when I'll be able to get another full night's sleep?"

It was Annie's turn to roll her eyes. "Honestly, Hannah, you're ridiculous. Here we are, on the verge of our final semester of college. We've worked so hard and we'll be out in the world before we know it, but you can't even let yourself enjoy it."

"You don't call this enjoying it?" I raised my own cup of booze.

"No, I mean we should go out."

"You know I hate that. I can never enjoy myself."

"You never let yourself! You're such an amazing person. You're allowed to have a little fun in your life, you know? And besides, in a year, you'll probably turn completely to your homebody ways. Let me get at least one more night of fun with you."

She waggled her eyebrows at me. I sighed at her and flipped my hair over my other shoulder, thinking back. Annie and I had come a long way from the tiny babies we were when we'd first met as college freshmen. I was so awkward then. It didn't help that I had just moved miles from my small hometown in Pennsylvania to the den of wonder and sin that is New York City. I was studying journalism and it felt like everyone in my classes wanted to jump in front of speeding trains and cut their way through thick jungles just to get the best story. All I wanted to do was write about fashion, film, and all the glamorous people living in the glittering city.

Sure, I had fun. And with my work accumulating, there wasn't an internship I wanted that I didn't get. But, looking at it now, I was struck by how lonely those first years had been. Maybe I'd come off as standoffish, or maybe I'd just been too shy, but I hadn't made many friends during those years.

Except Annie, of course. She lived down the hall from me in the dorms. Those nights that I'd be sitting up, writing and researching for hours, Annie would knock on my door with a boisterous smile and a six pack from the bodega around the corner. Just before our junior year we moved out of the dorms and into a tiny two-bedroom apartment. All the while, Annie would drag me to parties and adventures with her parade of friends that she somehow made everywhere she went. Between her red hair and sparkling green eyes, and my brown on blue, we always attracted attention.

"If I show up to class tomorrow hungover, it'll be your fault."

"Yay, senioritis!"

"I'm serious. And so broke! I still need to find a job for this semester."

"Only you would give yourself a completely full course schedule for your last semester and also try to take a job while doing it. Come on. You know you want to ..."

Folding my laptop and putting it aside on my bed, I walked over to the wing-backed chair next to my window. It was one of the only things I'd splurged on when I'd first moved out of the dorm. Not even my mattress was as comfortable. I liked to sit there and stare out the window at the shining stars and city below. I sighed, my breath slightly fogging the window for a second.

"Honey, you need a man," she informed me, not for the first time. Annie was moderately obsessed with my love life.

"It's not that I wouldn't like one," I replied. "I just ... it's never right, you know?"

"No, I don't know," she replied. "Did you study journalism or poetry? Because I know about all your big dreams about the perfect romance, but that stuff isn't real. If you want to find someone to hang out or okay, fine, fine, to spend your *life* with, you have to go through a few duds first."

I shrugged. "Maybe it sounds silly ... but I can't help what I want. Sparks and all."

"You're picky. I get it." Annie got up and held my hands in hers. For all her teasing, I knew that she cared about me and wanted the best for me. "No random one-night hookups, then. But we still deserve a party. Why not go out there and make them want us a little bit?"

I smiled and looked back out at the city. New York had always symbolized a new beginning to me; a world of endless possibilities. And maybe Annie was right. Maybe I had been so focused on my studies that I'd hardly made any room for life and passion. Who knew where I'd be in a year? Maybe, at least a little bit, I could grab the world by the horns while I still had a chance.

"I don't know how, but you've convinced me to have yet another night of debauchery," I said.

"Hurray to bad influences!" Annie cheered. "Now, finish your drink so I can do your makeup. We're going to do the night right."

CHAPTER TWO

The club was abnormally crowded for a Sunday night. Apparently we weren't the only ones looking to have a final hurrah before the semester started. The dance floor was absolutely packed. Go-go dancers danced as the DJ mixed his tracks on the stage above, surrounded by an all-chrome turntable. The crowd and smell of sweat reminded me why I usually avoided clubs like this at all costs. But the music was thumping and I was feeling the drinks from earlier as I danced with Annie.

A small but dynamic man approached us with two drinks and a huge smile. He made eye contact with my breasts before he did with my eyes. I could already feel the eye roll coming on. And the creeps, I thought. I didn't come to clubs much, and one big reason was the creeps. They lived in the walls, apparently.

"Good evening, ladies," the stranger rumbled. "Hope you're having a fun time."

"The best!" Annie responded, throwing him her most charming smile.

"The drinks are compliments of my friend over there," he continued, gesturing to a man leaning against the bar, who raised his own drink at us. "He was wondering if you'd like to join us at the bar."

Annie turned to me and raised her eyebrows. "Would we?"

I shook my head. "You two go right on ahead. I'm enjoying myself here."

A flash of concern and sincerity crossed her face. "Seriously?"

I nodded, genuinely wanting her to enjoy herself too. "Sure, have fun! I am."

Annie nodded before threading her arm through the stranger's and walking up toward the glowing wall of liquor at the bar. I continued dancing, lost in my own bliss and enjoyment of the moment. I spend my life planning for things and thinking about the future. I like to seize moments like this, when I am completely and purely living in the now. I let the music flow through me and the rest of the club patrons drifted away. I didn't think about how much my feet were killing me in those heels or what I looked like to other people. It was so freeing. In a way, I was happy Annie wasn't even with me in that moment. I was able to have some pure, alcohol-fueled fun, away from the sight of anyone who knew me.

I was nodding my head back and forth to the music when I opened my eyes and saw him.

There was a man dancing a few yards away from me. The first thing I noticed was he was absolutely stunning. He was wearing a dark button-down shirt, which pulled slightly over his strong arms and broad shoulders. I had never before seen someone wear jeans so well, and as he moved his hips, I couldn't draw my eyes away from his round, perfectly sized ass. His skin seemed to glisten and change colors in time with the beat and flashing lights on the dance floor. He had medium-length blonde hair with a slight curl to it; the roots dark with his sweat.

His clean-shaven, square jaw framed out one of the most handsome faces I'd ever seen.

He was also dancing alone. I wondered who he'd come here with.

And just as I was about to look away and blush at the thought of ogling a complete stranger, he looked up and we made eye contact. His eyes were crystalline blue, like a clear, open sky or the perfect Caribbean water. I swallowed hard. For some reason, I felt the sudden need to chug a gallon of water or find the ripest apple in a bunch and sharply bite into it, letting the juice run down my chin. He smiled at me as his eyes watched my throat move.

And then he was moving through the crowd toward me, and I could swear that each one of his footsteps was in time with the frantic beating of my heart.

I was expecting the usual kind of treatment that I got from men in clubs: a gruff grab by the hips, a whisper in my ear promising more, an indelicate dance designed to fuck me through my clothes. Instead, he reached out and gingerly took my hand in his as if it were made of precious porcelain, then gently pressed his lips to the back of my palm. I wanted to laugh. What am I, a princess? But I couldn't bring myself to. The gesture itself was corny, but somehow extremely touching. Very few men in this world could make you feel like an absolute queen in the middle of a sweaty club...

He looked up. "What's your name?" he said in a dark baritone.

"I'm Hannah," I managed.

"Hannah," he repeated. I felt my whole body clench in anticipation when he said my name. I'd never heard anything like it before. "My name is Austin," he replied.

"Hey," I said inarticulately.

"Mind if I ask you to dance with me? I saw you from across

the room, and I ... well, I absolutely had to try to at least meet you," he said, with a surprising level of sincerity.

"Of course," I said, sliding my hands over his shoulders. Dancing was good. Dancing, I was comfortable with. Dancing, I could handle.

Except I'd never danced with Austin before. The beat thumped through my chest and into his. He was an amazing dancer and he made me feel like we were sharing the same breath. His hands slid up my arms and his fingers slowly glided over my collarbone. He traced thin lines down my sides to my hips, where his hands burned prints into my skin through my form-fitting dress. I could feel my whole body leaning into his, and I thought he might even have been supporting my whole weight in his hands. I was usually a bit of a clumsy dancer in couple's dances, but somehow my feet knew exactly where to go. Dancing with Austin felt incredible and natural. Before I knew it, the song was over.

I was about to mourn the loss of his touch when he leaned in and whispered into my ear.

"Stay with me for the next song?" he murmured.

"Yes." The response came out of me like a sigh. What was it about him? He drew my desire out like poison from a wound.

"Good," he whispered as he drew me closer. "Because I'm not even close to being done with you."

As the deep bass of the next song began, Austin drew me against him, our hips flush and our knees rubbing together as we swayed. This was too intimate... which simultaneously thrilled me and terrified me. This was something I was not comfortable with ... but I couldn't stop.

And then I felt it. I felt his cock pressed up against me through the leg of his pants. I gasped at the contact, but I didn't feel ashamed or shy by it. I moved my leg against him experimentally, and I felt more than heard him moan against me. I pressed my face against his shoulder to hide my blushing. He took it a step further when his hands slid down my back and landed on my ass. He massaged me lightly for a moment, in wide, flat-palmed circles, but then he gripped me, roughly pressing and kneading me, guiding my hips up and down the shape of his cock, positioning himself directly up against the already soaked front part of my panties.

I'm going to cum like this, I realized. I was so turned on, so ready to go, and I could feel him beginning to pick up the pace, getting me closer and closer and ... then he stopped. I was sure he heard my groan of frustration. I pulled slightly away, flushed and flustered, to glare up at him for teasing me. He chuckled in response.

I was so worked up, I barely noticed when he withdrew one of his hands and lifted it to my face. With a finger, he traced my jawline and drew my eyes up to his. I could see the kiss coming from a mile away. His eyes filled with dilated, aroused pupils as he leaned in, waiting for me to stop him. "Trust me, I want to make you fall apart tonight," he breathed against my face. "But I won't do that until I've done this first."

I didn't stop him. From the first moment his lips brushed mine, the kiss exploded. His lips were soft, testing the waters, but skilled and purposeful. Mine were more than happy to follow his lead. Our hands were all over the place, roving over our bodies, and our mouths danced, unaware of the music or the people around us. I moved my hands over his arms, feeling the warm muscles twitch underneath my fingers. I caressed my way down his chest to feel his pecs – his nipples small and hard through his shirt – and made my way down what was clearly a tight, toned stomach. Then he pulled away and whispered in my ear again.

"Come home with me."

Like a glass window, it felt like the world around me shattered. The words were a bucket of cold water to my ecstasy. I jumped back from him as if he were on fire, eyes wide. He held my hands, concern in his eyes.

"Hey. You don't have to if you don't want to. I was just asking."

He reached forward and pushed a strand of hair behind my ear. It was a surprisingly tender gesture for the middle of a dance floor, and I found myself leaning my face into his palm. I kissed the tips of his fingers, lightly biting down on his thumb.

"Hannah!"

I whipped my head toward the sound of my name, and Austin snapped his hand away. It was Annie, waving at me from the other side of the dance floor with her arm wrapped around the man from the bar. God, I'd almost completely forgotten that I was out with her.

"Come on!" she screamed. "These guys know the best place to get a burger nearby!"

I turned back to Austin. He looked strangely downcast, as if he wasn't going to go find a new person to dance with the minute I left. The thought made me feel strangely sad too.

"I should go," I murmured.

"Can I at least get your number?" he asked.

I bit my lip. "Got a pen?"

He pulled a red marker out of the back pocket of his pants. At my raised eyebrow, he chuckled. "I carry these everywhere I go. Weird, I know."

He pulled back his sleeve to show me the pale inside of his lean arm and handed me the marker. I wrote down my number as legibly as possible and handed the marker back. He held my hand and the marker for a moment, stroking the top of my hand with his thumb. I exhaled and looked up. His eyes held the promise of everything he wasn't able to do to me tonight. Finally, he released my hand. He smiled, winked at me, and disappeared, swallowed by the throng of dancing bodies.

I WAS GETTING ready for bed and chugging a massive water when Annie came back into my room.

"So, are you going to tell me about tall, blond, and dance-y yet?"

I rolled my eyes. "I'm just trying to get into bed here."

"You two looked very cozy ..." she teased. "I hope you got his number or something. Things looked positively electric between the two of you."

"I gave him mine." I smiled at her, raising my eyebrows.

"Good. Goodnight, honey!"

She floated out the doorway the same way she came. When I was finally in bed with the lights turned off, my phone lightly buzzed. I opened it up to a text from an unknown number.

I'm sorry our time together was cut short. It was amazing meeting you tonight. -- Austin

I fell asleep with a smile on my face.

THE SMILE DIDN'T LAST. I felt like the dead the next morning. It was a beautiful, crisp winter morning, but I found myself completely unable to enjoy it. I could barely stand being in line for coffee. I checked my watch. Ten minutes until class was supposed to start ... I was cutting it close. The only saving grace of that morning was Austin and I had been texting nonstop.

I could tell he was not looking to play games with me. He was a guy who knew what he wanted. The texts were definitely flirty, but nothing too racy or overt. I preferred it that way. I was a writer. I did like a little bit of innuendo. Plus, things had already gotten so steamy between us on the dance floor the previous night. I was re-reading our most recent text exchange when the roar of the barista raised over the crowd.

"Hannah!"

I jumped, and my headache wailed in response. I glared at the hapless sophomore holding my coffee and snatched it up from him. I half walked, half jogged to the lecture hall, terrified the professor would beat me there. I arrived in a mostly full, professor-less room and sighed in relief. Taking a big, relieved swig of my coffee, I found an empty seat in the middle of the room. I opened my notebook and started to draw some flowers in the corner of the page. I couldn't help that I had to doodle on every piece of paper I saw. I checked my watch again. Even my professor was five minutes late. I went back to my doodling. Eventually, I could hear the door of the lecture hall swing open and a hush fell over the room. Biting my lip, I didn't look up, but concentrated on a leaf shape I was shading in. My ears rang when a familiar voice floated across the room.

"Sorry I'm late. Long night. It looks like many of you had the same."

A small laugh floated around the room. My knuckles turned white as I gripped my pen. No ...it couldn't be.

"Let's jump into it. My name is Dr. Parks and I'll be your professor for Victorian-Era Poetry and Literature. But since we're trying to get to know each other, you can call me Austin."

My head snapped up, and there he was, leaning against the desk at the head of the lecture hall in a flattering button-down shirt, not unlike the one he'd been wearing the night before. His blonde curls were under slightly better control, though, and his hair looked lighter than ever in the daytime. He shuffled a few papers on his podium and pulled a red marker out of his back pocket to mark them up. He cleared his throat and looked up. There was absolutely no mistaking him as his clear blue eyes locked onto mine.

CHAPTER THREE

Standing just inside the door with it locked behind me, her face played in front of my eyes as though my mind was making up for my refusal to look at her throughout the class.

Hannah Cosgrove.

I knew her full name now from the class roster. God, she'd driven me insane when we'd danced together in the club. She'd seemed so confident, so uncaring of anyone else's concerns as she danced alone. But there was something gorgeously pure about her, like fresh, uncut grass or a smooth beach, unmarred by footprints. Beautiful and untouchable. I had to make her mine. I couldn't tell if I had offended her or shocked her when I'd invited her back to my place. And then she'd had to leave with her friend. This was not my first time around the block, but I couldn't help the small voice that was urging me on, insisting that it had never felt like this before.

I'd come to work that morning feeling hungry and hungover, so I'd had to do a double take when I'd seen her sitting almost directly in front of me, looking just as shocked as I felt.

She was my student, of course.

I couldn't get involved now, no matter how much I wanted to. And, God, did I want to. She was gorgeous, magnetic, and absolutely enticing. But it was also too great a conflict of interest. It would put us both at risk. So I was going to have to avoid her at all costs.

She also deserved better than someone who had as much baggage as I did. Danny, my son ... I could never think of him as baggage, of course not. I loved him. I tried to be as good a dad as I could be, given the circumstances. My ex-girlfriend, Vanessa, got pregnant shortly after we graduated high school. I had already left for college, and she'd kept the pregnancy from me for several months. Needless to say, the relationship hadn't lasted long. But Danny had been born on Valentine's Day the next year, and from then on, he had been my world.

He split his time between Vanessa and me, staying with her when I was at school and staying with me while she was working. Vanessa had gotten a job at the local news broadcasting company and worked her way up to being one of the regional correspondents. Meanwhile, I'd worked shit jobs, bussing tables and slinging coffee while I earned my B.A., M.A., and Ph.D. I'd finally gotten to the point where I could do what I wanted to do the most: teach. It was hard for me to believe that Danny was nearly eight now.

I loved Danny and wouldn't trade him for the world. I made some stupid decisions when I was young; some of which I deeply regretted. But I didn't regret him. But I also couldn't ask a student of mine to violate the university rules, be with me, and take on a single dad with a seven-year-old. I knew that no one wanted to deal with that at her age.

But I was still so keyed up from seeing her ... so shocked, so revolted at myself, so ... turned on. The mere sight of her did things to me. My fear of being cornered by her after class dissolved swiftly into desire. I had to struggle all the way through my first lecture, simultaneously trying to do my job and resisting the urge to pull her out of her seat and kiss her like last night.

I sat at my desk for a moment, running my hands through my hair over and over again before eventually relenting and picking up my phone, dialing Leo's extension. It rang twice before he answered.

"Humanities department, this is Leo Renuard."

"It's me."

"Austin! Hey! I wanted to call you. I lost you at the club last night. What happened?"

I started bobbing my knee up and down anxiously. "There was this girl ..."

"Ooh! Scandalous!"

"No, shut up. Listen. I came to class this morning and it turns out she's one of my students."

Leo snorted. "So what?"

"So what?" I repeated in disbelief. "She's my student. Hello? Ethics?"

I could hear him rolling his eyes. "They're in college, Austin. They're adults. We run into them around the city. It's not like you knew she was a student when you were on the dance floor. It happens."

"It doesn't happen to me!"

"With your track record, that's hard to believe."

"She's just ... she's so different." I groaned. "What do I do, man? I can't teach like this. I can't get her out of my mind."

"Listen. You're imagining this person you wanted once on the dance floor. And she's so perfect. She's so sexy that you can't believe how much you want her. But once you realize how young she is, how she's just a person at school, you'll move on. Just try to view her through that mentality. She's just a kid, Austin. A legal kid, but nonetheless. Ultimately, young and naïve and not nearly as interesting as someone your own age with some kind of life experience."

"When you put it that way ..." I sighed. "You're right, you're right."

"She's just a girl, Aussie."

"I know. And my name is Austin."

"Let me live. I'm trying new things over here. Want to get lunch?"

CHAPTER FOUR

"What do you mean I can't drop the class?" I paced the room. Annie pretended not to laugh, sitting in my chair by the window. I gave her a warning look.

"Well, I have to get out of it somehow. There must be another ... okay. Okay, fine. Fine!" I angrily hung up and flung my phone across the room. I flopped down onto my bed, burying my face in the pillow.

"So?"

I turned my face. "I need the credit to graduate on time and all the other classes that satisfy it are completely full."

"Oh, boo hoo, you have to stay in class with Professor McHottyface."

"I'm so glad you find this hilarious."

"Hey," Annie got on the bed next to me. "It's like I was saying the other day. It's your last semester. Maybe now's the time to really go for it, you know?"

"I don't, actually. Go for what?"

"You know what. He's hot and he's clearly into you. Why the heck not?"

"He's my professor."

"He's also a red-blooded man who has needs. And you have needs too! Even if you like to pretend that you don't."

She patted my back. I snorted. It reminded me of my grandmother.

"I have a lunch date so I have to go. You know, though, Hannah ... just think about it."

I didn't acknowledge when she left. I simply waited to hear the sound of my door click closed. I rolled onto my back, staring at the ceiling. I found myself wondering about what Annie had said. I had played it so safe all through college, and now that I thought about it, all through life. Maybe it was time for me to really go there. Whatever I chose, he was stuck being my professor. I had to just deal with it. And, unfortunately, dealing had to happen soon, because as it turned out I had his class in like ... five minutes.

"Shit!" I bolted out of bed as I saw the time, grabbed my books and booked it out of the dorm at top speed.

TURNED out class with Austin flew by. He was a really great teacher, and I could say that even though half the time I was listening with one ear while simultaneously watching Austin's mouth as he read aloud. He was wearing his glasses again. Damn those things. I didn't notice he needed them at all until he put them up on his nose to read to us from a book. I found it simultaneously adorable and endearing. He pushed them up his nose and licked his lips as he turned the page. And that made me remember his taste ...

"I remember, I remember," he recited, cutting into my thoughts but not making things better as he recited poetry in that gorgeous voice. "The fir trees dark and high; / I used to think their slender tops / Were close against the sky: / It was a childish ignorance, / But now 'tis little joy. / To know that I am farther off from heav'n / Than when I was a little boy." As he closed the book, you could almost hear the audible sigh from all the women in the lecture hall. He looked up at us and smiled.

"Who can tell me what they think Mr. Hood is referring to when he writes this poem? Simple nostalgia? Or possibly something more?"

The lecture hall was silent. "Really, nothing? I was hoping I would get at least a little more than that," he suggested with a wiggle of his eyebrows.

A giggle passed over the room. He checked his watch. "We're five minutes over anyway. Go home and think on it. If we have silence again on Thursday, I'll start calling people out and I know how you guys feel about that."

What? Time to go already? I stared at the clock in shock.

A nervous chatter. Students began packing up and filing out of the room. I rushed to collect all my things. But just as I was hastening toward the door, I heard my name.

"Hannah."

I stopped hard in my tracks. I turned painfully slow toward him. I had completely forgotten the effect of hearing him speak my name. My knees were already shaking.

"Could you hold on for a second?"

"Y-yes," I stuttered, and he smiled and moved to address a few students who had questions.

When the room had finally emptied completely, Austin turned towards me, and just like that, the electrical connection re-awoke. I could nearly hear it humming in the air. I braced myself for what would happen next, and was surprised when he finally spoke.

"I think there's another class coming in here. Would you mind walking with me to my office?"

The words were so casual, so innocuous, so ... innocent, that

I actually laughed in response. He smirked at me and rolled his eyes to himself. I could tell we were at least on the same page about how awkward it was to be discussing office hours with someone who had had their tongue down your throat barely a week ago.

"Yes, sure," I finally responded.

"Great. Follow me."

We walked in silence across the campus. I tried to distract myself by observing the world around me, musing at the campus being part city, part college campus, and reflecting on the times I had had in this spot or the other. I still couldn't believe I was only a couple of months away from it all being over. I did this only to ignore the voice in my head urging me to grasp his hand in mine, pull him in, and restart our kiss from the nightclub.

We reached the academic building and didn't stop until we were inside his modest, private office. It was a very tasteful, yet masculine, setup. The walls were absolutely covered in yards and yards of books. His desk was a deep-colored wood with a rich, comfortable-looking leather chair right behind it. In front of the desk sat two inviting chairs facing the window behind it. He didn't seem to have a computer, until I noticed the laptop folded discretely on the corner of the desk.

"You can sit down," he murmured, and I wondered for an alarming second whether or not he could read my mind. I nodded and sat down, crossing my legs and folding my hands in my lap. Austin rounded the desk and sat down, leaning forward immediately.

"Let's just address the elephant in the room, because I know that it's making us both uncomfortable," he began. My mouth felt suddenly very dry. "We met for the first time at a club and ... we did more than just dance."

I would have been surprised if the blush didn't reach my

toes. My silence apparently prompted him to continue to speak. "Now, I think that at this stage, there's no point in denying the fact that I'm attracted to you. You've even felt the evidence of that." This remark elicited an audible gasp from me.

Austin chuckled darkly. "But, obviously, our positions as student and teacher in an academic setting must take precedent and I can't act on these feelings." I nodded much more than I had to. I was strangely disappointed to hear this. I knew the rules. I was not sure what I expected. Maybe I had had a small glimmer of hope that now would be the moment we both decided to break the rules. I think more than anything, I was trying to nod through my nervousness. Austin let out a nervous laugh of his own.

"You're allowed to talk too, you know," he commented.

"Sorry," I blurted out. "I'm ... sorry. This is just too weird."

"I agree," he continued. "I just wanted to clear the air. I want you to feel comfortable in class and know that I'm there to be your teacher. I don't want you to think that you can't talk to me or think that you need to avoid me because we had an ... encounter before we knew who the other was." He swallowed harshly. "And I'm sorry if anything I did the other night upset or offended you. I think I got a little demanding, carried away, and I'm sorry for all that."

My eyes widened. This was a different approach. I wasn't expecting this. But I wouldn't forgive myself if I let him continue to think that I was upset by his actions. "Don't apologize for that, please. I actually ... I liked it. I liked it a lot." I could feel myself blushing again at my inability to piece together my words. I looked up to see his eyes darken. He made a low sound in the back of his throat. Had he just growled?

"Don't say that to me. You're not allowed to say things like that to me," he said, barely above a whisper. A beat passed between us where I was sure we would say damn it all to the rules and he'd drag me into his arms, when the phone suddenly shattered the moment. We both jumped at the sound. He cleared his throat, loosened his tie, and picked up the phone.

"Hello? Oh ... he's here now? Yes, of course. Don't leave him standing out there. Let him in."

He hung up the phone and I looked up at him curiously. "Should I go?"

"Only if you want to. Please don't leave on my account. But we will have a visitor: my son, Danny."

"Oh," I said. My eyes instinctively went to check his wedding band ring finger for probably the hundredth time and I saw the same thing as always. It was a bare-naked finger. The thought made me blush a moment as I considered what a "bare-naked Austin" might look like, but the thought was gone as fast as it came. My boldness made Austin laugh uncomfortably.

"Yes, you're correct. No wife."

"Divorced?"

"Not exactly. We were young."

We barely had a moment for the awkwardness of the situation to sink in before his office door burst open on a flurry of blond hair and childhood enthusiasm.

"Dad!"

"Hiya, peanut!" I watched as Austin scooped up his son into his arms for a massive bear hug that the kid seemed to enjoy for a second before realizing he was 'too cool' and scrambling down. Chuckling, Austin ruffled the boy's hair. "I missed you, bug. Bug, meet Hannah. Hannah, this is my son, Danny."

"Hi, Hannah!" Danny said, flashing me a smile devastating enough to rival his father's.

"Hi, Danny. Nice to meet you. How old are you?"

"I'm turning eight!"

"Wow. Congratulations!"

"Thanks."

"What grade are you in school?"

"Second. I get all A's in math," he informed me. "And I like trucks and planes."

"Sounds like we've got a little engineer here."

"That's what my dad always says." He rolled his eyes so endearingly that I grinned.

"Give me just a sec, Danny," Austin said. "Hannah's one of my students. We're just here for a quick meeting." He turned to me. "I'm sorry about this. His mother and I both work, and I still need to hire a sitter for the new semester."

My ears pricked at that. "A sitter? I could do that."

Something unreadable flinched in his face. "Really?"

Hannah, what are you doing?

"Yeah. I mean, I need a job," I blurted, before the voice of reason that had always held me back before could take over now. "And you'll have to find someone to watch him when we're both in class but ... otherwise, I can help out whenever you need." I ignored that insistent voice that warned this was the worst idea ever. In place of that voice, I heard Annie. *Take a chance, Hannah. Just for once in your life, don't play it safe.*

He studied me. "You're sure you'd be all right with that? I could really use the help. If you're uncomfortable, please don't say yes just to be nice."

With one final shove, I kicked my usual caution to the curb. "It's no trouble at all. I'd love to do it."

His smile lit up his cozy office. "Well, great. I'm glad to hear it. So ... how about we do a playdate with you two tomorrow so you can meet and we can see if you're a good fit?"

I nodded enthusiastically. "Sounds perfect. What do you think, Danny? Do you want to go on a playdate with me?"

"Do you like cars?" he asked with comical uncertainty. I was, after all, a girl.

"I don't know much about them, but you can teach me," I replied.

"I can try," Danny agreed, and I bit back a smile at his solemn tone.

Austin cleared his throat. "And in regards to the meeting, you're sure you're okay with this? With me being your professor? We're all good?"

I returned the grin. "Peachy keen."

CHAPTER FIVE

I downed my third whiskey sour before finally saying it out loud. "She's going to be babysitting my kid starting tomorrow."

Leo looked up from his own drink. "Who?"

"Hannah."

"Hannah ...?"

"My student," I reminded him.

"Ah." He cracked his knuckles. "Not quite the approach I suggested you take, I don't think."

I rubbed my temples and flagged down the bartender for another drink. "I tried to. I swear. Every minute I spend with her just makes me want her more. Tomorrow is the test run, but she met him when he came to my office today. I know she'll do great. He's already taken with her."

He gave me a look. "Sounds like he's not the only one."

I glared at him as I got my new drink and immediately downed half of it. "That's not funny."

"Take a joke. Meanwhile, you just need to hook up tonight. You know? Forget her, move on. She can't possibly be that amazing."

"Except ..." I chugged more of my drink. "Except, she is."

Leo suddenly slammed his drink against the bar, sloshing beer over the sides. I jumped in surprise. He had a look on his face that I'd never seen before.

"You don't need this drama in your life and you certainly don't need to be falling in love with a student."

"Love?" I sputtered in shock. "Who said anything about love? Why would you bring that up?"

"It doesn't matter if it's love or not. You're too hung up on her. She seems perfectly nice, but you've got a grown-ass life to live."

"I'm not hung up on her. I'm having a brief ... infatuation."

"Alright, then," Leo challenged. "Prove it. Go take that girl home." He pointed at a tall, beautiful, but decidedly not-Hannah woman leaning against the wall on the other side of the bar. I rolled my eyes.

"I can't take any random girl I choose home, Leo. In case you forgot, that's not how anything in life works."

"Sure, you can't. But you can take home someone who's looked at your ass three times already tonight and you've been too busy feeling sorry for yourself to notice."

I looked back over towards the woman on the wall to find that Leo was right. She was still looking at me. She really was beautiful. Long raven hair, quicksilver eyes and a sly, flirty smile. She was older than Hannah. In fact, the two looked a lot alike ... almost like looking into a picture of Hannah in the future. I finished my drink. I could do this. I could be with her tonight. I couldn't deny that I was attracted to her.

I stood up and straightened my shirt, clearing my throat. "Hold my seat," I told Leo as I headed across the dance floor, automatically recreating the moment that Hannah and I had laid eyes on each other. With her body moving to the sound of the music, my body couldn't help but be drawn to hers like a magnet. When we touched, danced, breathed each other's air, I felt higher than any drug could ever make me.

"Are you going to ask me to dance or just stand there with your jaw hanging open, looking like an idiot?"

I shook my head, clearing my thoughts, as I looked up. The gorgeous brunette was standing directly in front of me, giving me a little smirk and a raised eyebrow.

"You don't look like you really think I'm an idiot," I suggested, the suaveness resurfacing in my voice. Her eyes flickered back up to mine, intrigued.

"I'm Marissa," she said.

"Austin," I responded. "Care to join me on the dance floor?"

"I was starting to worry you wouldn't ask."

I gripped her hand and led her to the center of the dance floor. Her hand was small and warm. But not soft like Hannah's ...

I shook my head again. *Give it a rest!* The booze I'd pounded away was really starting to affect me and I was no longer in control of my mind. I pulled Marissa's hips to mine and began to grind against her. She instantly moaned and bent forward and I couldn't help but moan with her. I ran my hands up her back, over her shoulders, up into her hair ... only it wasn't Marissa's perfume I was breathing in. Not Marissa's skin my hands were moving over. To the beat of the music, the name pulsed in my alcohol-stewed brain.

Hannah Hannah Hannah Hannah.

The room began to spin and I pulled back suddenly.

"Are you okay?" Marissa asked in surprise.

"Gotta go to the bathroom," was the only thing I could say as I rushed off the dance floor. My whole head was floating as I pressed into the bar's bathroom. Thank God, it had been cleaned recently and I pulled myself into an empty stall and locked the door behind me. I stared down at the toilet for a second, trying to decide if I was going to throw up or not. Being off the dance floor and in a well-lit room quieted most of my dizziness. I blinked and rubbed my eyes, trying to return myself back to the present.

What the hell was that back there? What was happening to me?

Visions of Hannah, a mixed bag of my own imagination and the small moments and touches we'd shared, filled my mind. The booze swam in my head, floating on a river of sexual frustration. I thought briefly of going back to the dance floor to collect Marissa for a quickie in the bathroom. But I knew that wasn't what I wanted. It was all wrong. The smell, the taste of her, her height, the exact color of her hair. None of it was right. The look Hannah had given me in my office earlier emerged in my mind, lips pressing together nervously, then the warmth in her eyes as Danny raced in.

My morality was fighting a losing battle. Despite the wrongness, awkwardness, and intensity of the situation, I couldn't turn away. I couldn't stop. I couldn't fight it.

Stumbling out of the stall, I slumped over, scrubbing my hands. For good measure, I splashed some water over my face, trying to clear my head.

Why couldn't I get this girl out of my mind? It was inappropriate, uncalled for, and I didn't need this in my life right now. I had come to the bar tonight thinking about the way she was looking at me when she agreed to babysit Danny, thinking about the tension between the two of us, determined to fuck her the next chance I got. But this was clearly something I couldn't shake. I couldn't even fuck anyone else, because I knew I just wanted her. But if I did that and threw caution to the wind just for her, I would risk everything. My job, my ability to support Danny, my reputation that I'd worked so hard for. Was she really worth all of that? Of course not!

I looked up at my reflection and decided that I hated Hannah Cosgrove. I didn't ... not really. But I couldn't afford to feel drawn to her anymore. It was too dangerous, and it made me act too reckless. I had to stay as far away from her as I possibly could.

But tomorrow she would be coming over to see if she was a good fit to be a sitter for my son. Fuck.

6

CHAPTER SIX

I rang the doorbell and adjusted my skirt, tugging it down with my hands. Annie and I had a twenty-minute conversation about what I should wear as I was trying to leave the apartment. I insisted that I was only going to test out if I was a good fit for this family, but she wanted me to wear something much more alluring. I flat out refused most of the outfits she pulled out for me, but we finally compromised on a long-sleeved shirt and a knee-length pleated skirt. Annie shoved me out the door, saying she'd be heartbroken if I didn't at least "tease Professor McHottyface a little bit."

Now, I was realizing just how short the skirt was. I'd pulled it down about a hundred times on the subway on my way over. I definitely felt out of place on the stoop of this fancy brownstone in some lovely part of Brooklyn. I couldn't remember the last time I'd visited somewhere so nice.

I was counting the panels on the wood door when suddenly it flew open and a disorganized-but-still-devastatingly-adorable Austin emerged. His hair was disheveled and wild around his face and his shirt was unbuttoned, revealing his white undershirt. He blinked, surprised to see me.

"Hannah, hi! Are you early?"

I frowned and checked my watch. "No? I think I'm just on time."

"Oh," Austin glanced at his own watch. "I must have lost track of time. Please, come in."

He ushered me into the apartment and closed the door behind me, hand hovering over the small of my back, but never touching. We paused in an elegant foyer with high ceilings and a small coat closet.

"Sorry I'm so unprepared. If it works out and you have to take care of a child, you'll get exactly what this whole situation is like." He laughed awkwardly.

"It's fine, please don't worry about it," I insisted. "I'm a guest in your home."

"Danny's just about finishing up his breakfast, so I'll show you into the kitchen."

Austin led me through the foyer, past a lovely staircase with a bannister painted white. The color seemed to be the theme of the apartment. White. Clean. Chic. Masculine. We entered a well-lit kitchen at the rear of the house with a large glass door facing a small backyard. The kitchen was clean with brand-new appliances. At an island in the middle of the room sat Danny, eating eggs and sitting on a tall bar-style chair. He was leafing through a comic book and looked up at the sound of us entering the room.

"Hi Hannah!" he said, smiling at me.

"Hey, Danny, ready for our playdate today?"

"Yeah! Dad got me a brand-new car magazine so I can teach you stuff!"

"Not so fast, bud," Austin interjected, and I caught the smile hiding in his eyes. "You've still got to change out of your pajamas, kid."

"Oh, yeah," Danny said, looking down at his Spiderman-themed jammies. "I'll be right back!"

Danny dashed out of the room, leaving his plate behind. I could hear his rushed steps pounding up the staircase. Austin gave me a self-deprecating smile as he picked up Danny's discarded plate and put it in the dishwasher.

"Seems like the teacher's going to become the student today," he said with a grin.

"I love to learn," I replied, then offered, "I can get that for you."

"Please, don't worry."

"I'm sure the breakfast cleanup is definitely part of the job," I reasoned. I walked around the island to take the plate from him, trying to convince myself that I wasn't just doing it to find an excuse to get closer to him. Our fingers brushed as I gripped the plate. Was that a sharp intake of air from him? I glanced up at him from beneath my eyelashes to glimpse his heated look. Smiling to myself in satisfaction, I turned to the sink, rinsing the plate and fork before bending to drop them in the dishwasher.

Closing the dishwasher door, I rose and was surprised to find that Austin was standing apart from me, on the opposite side of the island, as far as he could possibly get while still being in the same room. He had a possessed look on his face, troubled and stormy. I had sensed his dark mood from the moment I stepped in the door, but had to bite my tongue. It was so obvious in his body language, though, that I opened my mouth to say something, to see what could possibly be on his mind.

But I never had the chance. I barely had a word out before the sound of the front door opened and closed, surprising us both. The sound of heels echoed in the foyer.

"Hello? Anybody home?"

"Mom!"

Danny's rushed footsteps barreled down the stairs. Austin

frowned and moved into the foyer with an urgency I was sure I hadn't seen him move with before. I could feel my stomach drop to my feet as I cautiously followed him. In the foyer, Danny was embracing one of the most glamorous women I'd ever seen. She had long, impeccable legs, and was intelligently dressed in a perfectly matching and fitted skirt and top underneath this season's nicest winter coat. Her bone structure was insane. Feminine clavicle bones framed a long, swan-like neck, traveling up into the perfectly shaped-v of her jawline. High, royal-looking cheekbones sat above a pert chin and pouty lips. She had ice-cold blue eyes, deeply set underneath perfectly groomed brows. Flawless pale skin ended at a head of luscious blonde hair pulled back into a stylish knot at the back of her head.

"It's my baby boy! Hi, honey!"

"Mom, stop! I'm not a baby anymore!"

"Vanessa, what are you doing here?" I was alarmed at the tone of Austin's voice. There were equal parts shock and confusion, tinged with a little bit of anger. His crossed arms and frowning face spoke of his discomfort with the situation.

"What, I can't visit my son, say hi to my own flesh and blood?"

"You normally call."

"I had to talk to you about that, actually." Vanessa (as it appeared that was her name) turned suddenly and looked at me, as if noticing me for the first time, though I'd been there since Austin entered. "Oh, hello. Who are you?"

I cleared my throat and tried to put on one of my best smiles. "I'm Hannah Cosgrove. I'm one of Austin's students, and hopefully I'll also be babysitting Danny."

"I'm teaching her about cars!" Danny piped up proudly.

Vanessa's eyes flashed as she turned toward Austin. "First-name basis with the students, Austin? That seems very friendly," she said with a sarcastic and serious tone.

"I definitely don't prefer being called 'Mr. Parks' or 'Dr. Parks' all the time," he grimaced. It looked like every word to her caused him pain.

"I'm sure you don't," she said suggestively.

Who the hell did this woman think she was? Well, she was Danny's mother and Austin's ex ... whatever. But the way she had just come right on in and acted like she was in charge of the place didn't sit well with me. It apparently didn't sit well with Austin either. His face was pulled tight with tension, his eyes flashing from Danny to Vanessa, but tactfully avoiding mine.

"Anyway, I have an announcement," she said in a commanding voice. "I will be moving back to Brooklyn so I can be closer to the apple of my eye." She nuzzled Danny's face.

"Seriously?" Danny's eyes lit up.

"Seriously," Vanessa offered. Danny seemed thrilled, but I struggled to find a single thing that was warm about this woman. Everything was cold, from her voice to her smile.

"Vanessa, could we possibly talk in private?" Austin had asked a question, but it sounded more like a demand.

"What's there to discuss?" she asked. "There's nothing more to say. I'm just moving to be closer to him."

"When I got full custody..."

"Danny, can you go get your car magazine so you can start showing me stuff?" I asked, feeling bad for the kid and wanting to spare him the awkward tension between his parents.

Austin shot me a grateful look as Danny darted out of the room and Vanessa continued.

"I know we agreed that'd be best for Danny. It works best for us. And we agreed that I could continue to visit him and have a relationship with him."

"Yes, but moving ..."

"I won't be moving into the house with you!" She laughed, as if the idea was completely ludicrous. "I'll just be a five-minute walk away."

"You've already found a place?" Austin said skeptically.

"I've just made an offer. Fingers crossed they accept."

Austin chewed his lips. He didn't seem happy with any part of the situation. He looked like he was about to say something else when Danny ran back in, clutching his magazine.

Then Vanessa stepped in, and something like jealousy moved across her face. "Danny, you'll have hours with your babysitter. Why don't you take me upstairs first and show me any new robots you've gotten lately?"

"Cars, Mom," he corrected, but looking pleased at her unexpected interested. "Here, Hannah. You can look at it." He put the magazine on the table and they walked out of the room.

I turned to look at Austin, who seemed lost in thought.

"She seems … nice," I winced as soon as the words left my mouth. *She seems nice?* That was the best thing I could think to say? I felt better when Austin laughed slightly at the comment, lifting the mood. I felt bolder, and dared to ask the question that had been on my mind the minute I walked through the door.

"Are you and Vanessa … you know …"

Austin shook his head. "Not since Danny was born. Though, I'd hope you'd know that. No one trying to get back together with someone would dance the way you and I danced that night."

His mention of that night brought back the tension between us. It stole my breath away and I sharply inhaled, holding a moment before I felt I could release it. Austin clearly felt it too and coughed uncomfortably, casually walking across the foyer, again creating space between us.

. . .

ANNIE BURST OUT LAUGHING. I rolled my eyes and glared at her over the top of my coffee cup. "It's not that funny," I insisted.

"It has to be. It has to be funny, or else it's just sad," Annie insisted, wiping her eyes. "Of course he has a shitty ex! All the good ones do! Especially the ones with kids. Once you stick your dick in Crazy, there's no coming back from it."

"Do all the good ones also have an ex moving five minutes away to 'be closer to her son?'" I asked bitterly.

"No, but now you're starting to sound like a real bitch."

"I am not! Annie, how could you? You're my best friend."

Annie held her hands up in surrender. "Well, take a minute and think about what's really going on here," she insisted. "Austin has this child with her. Whether that was from a one-night stand or because they were so in love and thought they were going to be together forever doesn't matter and is, frankly, none of your business. They have this whole history together, and you don't know the situation. Is it possible she's trying to get back together with Austin? Sure, it is. Did he seem happy to have her there?"

I waited for a moment to see if the question was rhetorical before quietly responding. "No."

"Okay, well, then, if she is trying to get back with him, she's a bit far off from that goal. But it's also entirely possible that she did just move closer to be with her son, which is also completely valid and is her right. And here you are. You had this amazing night with Austin, but you honestly have no claim on him; you have no idea how he feels; and you're serving as a caretaker to his son. And you're also his student! So, I know you feel concerned, but you're jumping to conclusions. I guess what I'm saying is, chill out with the Vanessa thing and live your damn life."

"And what can I do about Austin? This shit between us ... it's ridiculous at this point."

Annie smirked. "As you know, I agree. Maybe just ask him what the deal is."

"You don't think that would be a little bit inappropriate?"

Annie snorted. "There's a lot about this situation that I wonder whether is appropriate," she snapped back.

"Fair point," I said, taking a sip of my coffee.

"What's your plan for the day?" she asked.

I groaned. I did not want to think about that at all. "I actually have an assignment due in Austin's class. A presentation on Lord Alfred Tennyson. I'm really nervous about it. You know how I get with public speaking."

Our freshman year, Annie had pressured me into trying out for the university's Shakespeare company. And though I loved Shakespeare and knew all my lines, at the audition I completely choked. I stuttered through the monologue and the moment I got off stage, I immediately ran to the bathroom and vomited.

"Oh, yeah, good times," Annie said. "You'll do great, though. It's just a class. And your extremely hot professor."

I rolled my eyes. "Thanks so much for the reminder." I glanced down at my watch. "I should get going."

"Me, too. I have work in a bit. Break a leg out there, Juliet!"

I stuck my tongue out at her as I grabbed my purse and headed out the door.

CHAPTER SEVEN

From the moment I walked into the lecture hall, my heart was racing. About half the class had already filed in, and Austin was there, listing the upcoming presenters on the board. I was number three. Good. Close to the top was good, because then I could get it over with and relax for the rest of the class. The anticipation would be over.

I paused inside the doorway, looking at Austin. He was wearing his glasses again, and looked as amazing as always; ass still filling out his paints, with a red marker sticking out of one of his rear pockets. He turned and noticed me standing there.

"Good morning, Hannah. Ready for today?"

I gulped and gave him my best effort at a smile. "Ready as I'll ever be."

He laughed. "I'm sure you'll do great."

My heart lifted a little. "Really?"

He looked at me, realizing I was serious about my nervousness. "Yes. I really do think you'll be amazing up there."

"Not just because I'm going to be taking care of your kid from now on?" I teased.

After Vanessa had left, the dark cloud that seemed to be

hovering over Austin lifted a bit. Of course, the day had gone spectacularly well. While Austin caught up on some emails, Danny spent an earnest 30 minutes trying to explain car parts to me, before giving up. So we went to the park instead and watched Danny as he crawled all over the jungle gym and whooshed back and forth on the swings. We spread out a small picnic blanket and shared some sandwiches.

When Austin ran to the water fountain to refill his water bottle, a passing heavily pregnant woman commented to me, "Cute partner and cute son. You must feel very lucky."

I smiled and didn't correct her. And I thought to myself that I did feel very lucky. I felt lucky for all of it.

"Hello? Hannah?"

I realized I'd zoned out and that Austin had been talking to me. "Oh. Sorry!"

Austin shook his head, smiling. "You don't know your own strengths. Give yourself some credit. I'm sure you'll blow us all away."

I smiled shyly at him before taking my seat. I returned, as always, to my nervous doodling. I tapped my foot all the way through the first two presenters, resisting an old compulsive urge to bite my fingernails. The anxious energy was building up everywhere in my body.

"Hannah Cosgrove."

My heart felt like it was about to beat out of my chest, and I couldn't tell if it was because Austin had spoken my name or my nervousness to stand up in front of everything. I made my way down the stairs to the front of the lecture hall, notes in my arms. I set my books down on the podium and cleared my throat. I took a breath.

"Lord ... Lord Alfred Tennyson..." I glanced up at the room full of uninterested faces. Some people were on their cellphones. My eyes flicked over to the desk where Austin was sitting with his rubric. He looked at me over the rims of his glasses and smiled at me encouragingly, nodding. I smiled back and took another deep breath.

"Lord Alfred Tennyson is a name I'm sure you're all familiar with, but his work speaks for itself."

And I was off.

It was incredible how at ease I felt delivering my report. The words fell from my lips like melted butter, so easily and simply. And whenever I got nervous, all I had to do was glance over at Austin, and I felt stronger knowing that he was on my side.

"'O love, they die in yon rich sky, / They faint on hill or field or river; / Our echoes roll from soul to soul, / And grow forever and ever, / Blow, bugle, blow, set the wild echoes flying, / And answer, echoes, answer, dying, dying, dying.' Many people would say that this poem is about the action of diminishing returns that comes with new love. But I interpret it as an appreciation of the power of those moments. These echoes reverberate for Tennyson because they're beautiful, even if they're brief. Tennyson knows that love is something to be cherished. Something worth fighting for."

I wrapped up my speech, waiting for something, anything to happen. I looked over at Austin. His heated gaze was enough to steal my breath and it must have shown on my face. He shook his head, schooling his features, and cleared his throat.

"Good job, Ms. Cosgrove. Very good. Mr. Craine?"

His attention was entirely on the next student as he began his report.

It was just past twilight when I arrived at Austin's brownstone, a sleeping Danny in my arms. He'd had Boy Scouts after school today, so I'd had to pick him up and make sure he made it home.

I had carried him the last block and a half after I caught him falling asleep while we were walking.

The house was locked and dark when I arrived. I was secretly relieved. Things between Austin and I had only been getting worse ... or better. I honestly couldn't tell. But the tension had completely gotten out of hand. After our moment during class, I really did not want to run into him tonight. It was a long day and I didn't have it in me to deal with the awkwardness between us, or his hot and cold treatment of me.

I trudged up the stairs and brought Danny to his room. I woke him up briefly to get him into his pajamas and have him brush his teeth. As soon as I tucked him in, he was completely out. I sighed and watched him sleep for a moment, yawning and fighting sleep myself. I turned off the lights and headed back downstairs.

I went into the kitchen, thinking I'd make myself a mug of coffee for the road. Nothing was worse than falling asleep on the subway. I was just closing the kitchen cabinet when I turned to see Austin standing in the kitchen's doorway. I jumped.

"Jesus Christ, you scared me! I didn't think anyone was home," I scolded him.

He didn't respond to me, just looked me directly in the eye. Was he breathing heavily? The attention made me fidgety.

"I hope you don't mind that I was making myself some coffee to take on the subway," I explained. "I'm feeling very sleepy and—"

I was cut off by Austin, who suddenly moved from the doorway, into the room. In four steps, he was directly in front of me, and he reached forward and joined his mouth with mine.

Well, now I wasn't sleepy at all.

My body responded to his instantly. I kissed him back and moaned, gasping for air between kiss after kiss. He grasped my hips and pressed me up against the counter, moaning when every inch of his body came into contact with mine. He moved his lips to my neck, kissing, sucking, and biting. I craned my head backward to give him more access and even in that moment of passion, my thoughts from earlier bubbled to the surface.

"What about ... What about the rules and ... God, that feels good," I moaned anew when he found a tender spot behind my ear.

"Fuck the rules. I'm done with them. I've been losing my mind trying to stay away from you, but I ..." His lips returned to mine and I whimpered. I couldn't believe how amazing it felt. "I'm going to do to you tonight what I should have done on the night we met. And the day after. And every day up until now that I didn't give us this, for the charade we've been playing."

His hungry hands ran up my arms and over the front of my chest, kneading my breasts roughly over my shirt and leaning down to kiss my shoulders, pulling the material aside for skin to skin contact. This time when I gasped, it was both out of surprise and out of pleasure. I'd never been touched there before. All of this was so new to me. His hands were so practiced and sure. I blushed at the thought. I had to tell him. I didn't want to, but if I didn't, he would find out eventually.

"Wait," I said, pulling away from him, even though every cell in my body was screaming, demanding that he and I be joined at once. The confusion and hurt on his face as he pulled away was evident, despite his best efforts to look open and compassionate. *He thinks I'm going to reject him,* I realized. While I was only worried that he would reject me. "There's something I need to tell you."

"Okay," he said, licking his lips.

I took a deep breath to steel myself. "I'm ... I'm a virgin."

His eyes widened in shock. "Seriously?"

I looked down and crossed my arms self-consciously. Austin

sputtered an apology. "Sorry, I ... I didn't mean ... There's nothing wrong with that. I'm just completely shocked. The way you are with me just makes it seem like this wasn't your first time. And you're so beautiful. I know that any young man would want you just as much as I do."

I sighed and stared down at my feet. "I know that's probably a lot of pressure for you, but I thought you deserved to know, because—"

Austin cut me off with a soft kiss. This kiss was different than the others we'd shared. Any other time Austin and I had kissed, it had been an insane collision of passion and fire, an extreme dance that felt on fire. This one was affectionate. It was physical reassurance, understanding, a way to say "I'm here with you." He pulled away and stroked my hair.

"I'm glad you told me," he began. "We're not going to fuck tonight."

I couldn't help the crestfallen look on my face. I wanted him. My body wanted him. I was sure I was already embarrassingly wet. But I shouldn't have been surprised that he didn't want me anymore. I knew the virgin thing might be a turn off. But at my saddened look, Austin chuckled and drew my eyes back up to his with a hand on my chin.

"You deserve an amazing first time. Candles, romance, the whole bit. Hannah, I just had you up against the kitchen counter and I would've taken you right here if you hadn't stopped me."

I bit my lip. "I was considering it."

Austin moaned and pressed his forehead against my shoulder. "God, do you have any idea what you do to me?" A tense beat passed between us. Austin seemed to be thinking of something. "Let me show you how much I want you tonight."

My jaw dropped. "But I thought ... you said ..."

"We're not going to fuck. But I want to ... unwrap you tonight."

I gave him a look for his choice of words. He smirked at me and leaned into my right ear. "Have you ever come so hard and so much that you feel like you've completely left your body?"

I was panting as if I'd run a marathon. All I could do was shake my head no. He began stroking his hands up and down the small of my back. "If you'd be open to it, to letting yourself come undone with me, I would love to have you."

I swallowed hard. This was it. I started nodding my head yes, but made sure I could verbalize, too. "Y-Yes. Please. I want that too."

Before I knew it, Austin had hitched me up in his arms, with my legs wrapped around his waist, and was carrying me towards the door. I squeaked quietly to myself and tightened my legs around him, holding on for dear life. I hardly had to. Austin's body was just as solid as I had imagined. I felt impossibly small and light in his arms. He carried me as if he was just moving a set of sheets between rooms.

As he mounted the stairs with ease, he whispered in my ear. "Danny could sleep through a stampede out his bedroom window." I giggled at the remark. "But we still have to take care with the screaming. We wouldn't want him to worry that anything was wrong."

I smirked at him. "Screaming? You're really hyping this, aren't you? It had better be as good as you say it is, otherwise I think I might be disappointed."

He smiled at me knowingly. "I promise you won't be."

We entered his bedroom. I hadn't snooped around in here yet, so I took a moment to observe my surroundings. There was a queen-sized bed at the center of the far wall, with an impeccable, inviting bedspread; a nightstand to the side with a small lamp; a closet next to the small dresser with a television perched overhead; the door to the master suite's bathroom; and a massive window from the ceiling to the floor, pouring moonlight into the room.

Austin walked me over to bed and laid me down gently, kissing me again. "Can I take your clothes off?"

I nodded nervously. It was one thing to think about it, but Austin asking to disrobe me like we were right out of a story and having him there in person wanting me and lying back on his bed was just too much for me. It was all so intense. Austin began with my top. He slowly peeled off my shirt, taking care to lay it on his dresser and continuing to touch and kiss every new piece of exposed skin. He trailed his hands back up to my bra, a hand covering each breast. He started teasing me through and around the thin lace material. His fingers traced the edges of the cups, dipping just slightly underneath to tease the tender flesh of my breasts.

I was lost to the sensation and I could feel my body moving in time with his circular motions, especially my hips as they ground against his thigh. He used his index fingers to trace my nipples through my bra, working them into tight, tender peaks. I was full-out moaning then, desperately seeking a release that still felt so far away. When he pinched my nipples through my bra, sending a jolt directly to my clit, I cried out and couldn't stand it anymore.

"Austin, take it off," I begged.

He grinned wickedly up at me and in a moment, his hand was unclasping my bra and wicking it away. He exhaled for a moment. "So fucking beautiful," he murmured before his hands came up to cover me again. His palms were intensely warm and arousing. He stroked the skin and worked my nipples with his fingers, but then he leaned down and took one of my peaks into his mouth. My hands flew to the back of his head to grip his hair and keep him there because it felt incredibly good. The variety of sensations were driving me insane. The wet flicks of his tongue, the harsh suction of his mouth, the singe of his teeth brushing me while his other hand massaged the neglected breast. He released me to speak.

"You feel close. Think you could come just like this, baby?"

I was incoherent. "I don't ... Maybe ..."

He dove back down to suck my nipple into his mouth, making me keen. But this time, he slung one of my legs over his shoulder and pressed his hips into me, grinding his hard dick down onto me. I moaned out loud. I couldn't believe how close I was just with some nipple stimulation and the best dry humping I think the world had ever seen.

"I think ... Oh God, Austin ... I'm close. I can't believe it, I'm fucking coming." He sped up his pace, doubling his efforts to finish me and then I came, turning into a puddle underneath him.

"Holy shit," he said. "Holy shit. That's the hottest, most amazing thing I've ever seen. You're so fucking responsive."

The echoes of the final waves of my orgasm had my head spinning. I whined, squirming uncomfortably in my jeans. Austin's hand descended down to the zipper fly. "I want to see what I've done to your pussy."

Despite my still-waning orgasm, the statement made me moan and shiver as Austin pulled my pants and underwear down in one go. Once they were off, Austin took another moment to let his eyes rove over my body and admire me. I realized that this was the first time I'd ever been naked in front of another person. Or at least, in a sexual context, not counting locker rooms. I was expecting to feel self-conscious in the moment. But the look on his face dispelled any doubts I might have had on what he thought of my body. He was still completely clothed, and I was now entirely naked. There was something so erotic and arousing about that. At the back of my mind, I recalled getting a wax recently and I silently thanked myself for that foresight. In fact, I wondered if I had made myself smooth because I was expecting him to take me at any moment.

Austin introduced his hands to me slowly, starting by massaging my legs up to my thighs, then tracing his fingers over the junction between the tops of my thighs and my pelvis, slowly drawing narrower and narrower paths until he was just gently teasing my outer lips. He gently spread me and dragged a single fingertip up the soaking length of me, from my entrance to my clit. My hips jolted off the bed in response, which he quickly corrected by using one of his forearms to pin me to the bed. I thought having another person touching me would be like when I touched myself, but the foreignness of Austin's fingers made the sensation feel five times as potent as I was used to.

"Do you ever touch yourself?"

"How do you like it? Slow and smooth?" He drew his fingers torturously slow over my clit, applying pressure, over and over again. "Or do you like it rough and fast?" He started rubbing my clit in frantic circles. A guttural sound emerged from me that I was sure I'd never made before.

"Both," I croaked.

I could've sworn I felt Austin growl as his attentions to my clit increased. I could feel myself chasing the peak again. So soon was completely unheard of. My body just couldn't get enough of him.

"Do you think about me when you touch yourself?"

I keened again, arching against his arm. I nodded again.

"What do you think about?"

I could feel myself blush at the question. "You," I responded.

"What do I do in your fantasies?"

This was more than new to me. I'd never been in a situation where someone was touching me like this or wanted me to tell them what I wanted sexually. I definitely found Austin's dirty talk very arousing, but I wasn't sure if I could do it, too. My feeble attempts so far had seemed to have the same effect on Austin that his words had on me, but I still felt a little self-conscious about the whole thing. I remembered what he had said earlier: that he wanted to unwrap me and he wanted me to be open with him.

Maybe that's what he was doing; trying to test my comfort zone and let me expose myself to him. I could refuse his encouragements if I wanted to, and I was sure he would respect that, but I didn't want to. There was no reason to feel shy. He was here with me, and I wanted to be here with him. I swallowed thickly.

"You touching me, fucking me with your fingers, and ..." I couldn't help but blush. "And your face between my thighs."

"God, really?" His pupils dilated to three times their size. Before I could respond, he was jumping off the bed and yanking me by my feet until my hips sat at the edge. In one swift motion, he was kneeling before me, like a man doing penance, throwing my knees over his shoulders. He used his hand to spread my lips and took one luxurious lick up the length of me. I cried out sharply, slapping my hand over my mouth to muffle the noise. Austin lifted his head.

"Like that?" he asked.

"Yes! Please, don't stop," I moaned as I grabbed onto his bedsheets for dear life. "I'm so close already."

The heat of his mouth on me was driving me insane, lapping over my clit again and again. My legs were shaking against his ministrations and spots began to develop behind my eyes. As the cherry on top of the sundae, his fingers replaced his tongue on my clit and he leaned down to gently insert his tongue into me, slowly fucking me with his tongue. Like that, the coil that had been winding within me snapped and I was flying. My thighs snapped shut, locking over his head, but he did not relent, stroking my body reassuringly as I came down from my high.

My legs went slack, falling loosely to the side. I thought that he was finally done with me. I lay there, completely spent. But then, Austin gently blew on my pussy, making me shiver, and returning his mouth to me, resumed softly penetrating me with his tongue. I shuddered.

"I can't ..." I struggled to get the words out. "I can't again. I'm too sensitive."

"You will," he assured, pulling his face away from me briefly. "And I'm not going to touch your clit at all this time. I want to see how much you can take."

I was about to ask him what he meant by that when he inserted one finger into me and began slowly moving in and out of me. His finger was thicker than mine, but it felt amazing.

"You feel so fucking tight."

He added a second finger and my breath hitched. I could definitely feel I was being stretched now.

"Oh, God ..." I moaned.

My enthusiasm spurred him on, and he started going faster and faster. I was riding his fingers with abandon and it felt incredible. But I wasn't quite there. My peak seemed slightly out of reach, no matter how hard he went. Suddenly, I felt him add a third finger.

"Oh, shit!" I yelped. The thickness was a heady sensation, with a twinge of discomfort. But before I could say anything, Austin began hooking his fingers inside of me after each thrust, pressing into a spot that felt like a pleasure button attached to every nerve in my body. I started moaning out of control.

"Hannah ... come for me, Hannah," Austin's flushed face murmured to me. "I want to feel you come for me again."

One, two, three thrusts later, I was thrashing my head into the bed, trying desperately to muffle my screams as my whole body shook with earth-shattering explosions. When I finally collapsed, I was panting and sweaty, lolling there blissfully, my body present but my head still stuck somewhere in the clouds. I didn't even notice Austin extricate himself from between my thighs and dress for bed.

The exhaustion from earlier was hitting me and I struggled to open my eyes when I felt him tucking my spent body into his bed. He spooned his body behind mine, holding my limp body and landing soft kisses on my shoulders and at the nape of my neck. I was struck suddenly when I felt him, still hard, pressed up against my ass. I fought sleep as I turned to look at him.

"But ... what about you ..." I was interrupted by a deep yawn. God, three orgasms really took a lot out of a woman. Austin just chuckled to himself.

"Another time. Tonight was just about you." He smoothed my sex-tousled hair back. "I was the first person to do any of those things to you, wasn't I?"

He kissed my lips and I could still slightly taste myself on his tongue. "Hm," he whispered. "That's delicious."

I settled into his arms easily. His cozy warmth lulled me to sleep swiftly. I leaned up one last time to press a kiss over his heart, then completely passed out, falling into a deep and sated sleep.

8
CHAPTER EIGHT

I woke up feeling content to the warmth of sunlight on my face. I couldn't remember my dream, but I knew that it was wonderful. I smiled and settled further into the plush pillow before being roused further awake by confusion. That wasn't my window. These weren't my sheets. This wasn't my bed. The sound of the shower running in the en suite bathroom brought me back to the present and memories from the night before flooded my mind.

I flopped onto my back, staring at the ceiling. Had that all really just happened to me last night? Had Austin really stripped me naked, carried me to his bed, and made me come harder than I ever had in my entire life? It all must have happened. Even I couldn't believe I'd have a fantasy that vivid, that intense. It must have all come true. And fuck, I had fallen into the deepest sleep I'd ever known in my life. What time was it? I craned my neck to look at the clock. Just after six in the morning. The sun must have just risen.

My attention was drawn again to the sound of the shower running. Austin. The night was absolutely amazing. I had to admit, I was a little disappointed that he hadn't ended up fucking me. I had been dreaming of being joined with him like that for weeks. I craved the feeling of his dick inside of me. I wanted to feel him within and without, making love endlessly until we had nothing left to give. But, oh, that morning, I felt truly fucked. The way he had brought me to completion and claimed every inch of me with his mouth. If anything, the whole ordeal made me want him more. I imagined him in the shower now, washing my scent from him, the warm water and suds of his soap running down his shapely body.

And then I began to wonder why I was just fantasizing about the whole thing when the real deal was just a short walk away ...

I licked my lips and sat up, realizing that I was still naked underneath the sheets. Blushing, I gripped the sheet to my chest, covering myself. But why should I be shy? He'd already seen everything. I rose, letting the sheet fall, and walked over to a full-length mirror hung on the back of his closet door. I inspected my own rested, flushed body.

I had never really given much thought to my body. I had no opinions about whether or not it was likeable or attractive. I always just viewed it as my body: something I was connected to, but was unwilling to qualify. Last night and the moments of shyness I had felt with Austin were completely new to me. I felt exposed in a completely new way. But the novelty of it, while it did frighten me a bit, was very arousing. And as I looked in the mirror at my naked body, I couldn't bring myself to look down on any part of myself that he had so enjoyed. In fact, I felt like Venus herself. A seductress. A sex goddess.

I seized this newfound confidence and took five confident strides to the bathroom, opening the door silently and entering. The interior of the bathroom was completely fogged up with steam from the shower, but that didn't stop my eyes from immediately being drawn to Austin. His bathroom was like the rest of his home: simple and chic. White, clean counter tops, a large vanity mirror, a jacuzzi tub in one corner and a shower in the other. The shower stall was all completely clear glass. He had his back to me as he rinsed out his hair in the spray, his perfect ass completely in sight.

I took a moment to admire him and remembered that I hadn't seen any of his nakedness last night. I observed the strong muscles of his back leading down into his beautifully formed glutes. His skin was pale and smooth and had the faint remains of last summer's swimsuit tan lines. His legs looked strong and sturdy, holding fast and flexing as Austin swayed slightly. I was shamelessly ogling him, and I didn't mind at all.

As soon as I thought I couldn't take it anymore and was about to enter the shower with him, he turned slightly, giving me the first view of his cock. Even limp and hanging between his legs, his size thrilled and terrified me. He was cut, with a small patch of groomed pubic hair above. I was clearly the furthest thing from an expert on dicks, but I knew enough to know that he had something to be proud of.

Austin's eyes suddenly opened, and seemed pleasantly surprised to see me there, catching me staring at his body. When our eyes met, the heat from the night before was instantaneously there, if not stronger.

"Good morning," he said. His voice was so shockingly tender and kind, in such a heated moment. He said it with a light tone, as if he'd run into me at the coffee shop, not caught me staring at his dick in the bathroom.

"Good morning," I replied. My voice cracked from disuse.

"If you want to take a shower too, I'll be out in just a minute," he assured me.

He wasn't dismissing me, but he wasn't demanding I join him either. The door was left open. Again, he gave me space to choose what I was most comfortable with. I didn't know much about the logistics of showering with another person, but I was sure that Austin and I could figure it out together.

I stepped forward, approaching the shower. I popped the door open and entered the shower, sealing myself in the warm cocoon that smelled like his shampoo. Austin was in contact with me almost instantly, holding me against him. He tenderly brushed back my now-wet hair and began laying small, tender kisses all over my face, neck, and lips. I sighed in contentment.

"Last night was ..." I began. "Amazing. Thank you so much."

"Thank you. I had a fantastic time. I'm sorry I basically mauled you ... I couldn't help myself with you."

I glanced up at him in mild annoyance. "Apparently, you could. You didn't want to fuck me."

"I think we both know that it wasn't a question of wanting." He thrust his groin up against my thigh lightly, letting me feel his growing erection. "But feel how crazy you make me? I can't even take you into my shower for a chat without my dick thinking this might finally be his day."

I giggled and pressed a kiss to his jawline. "So ... the virgin thing doesn't freak you out?"

"Not at all," he assured me. "I'm really glad that you told me. Otherwise I just would've taken you like that. You deserve more. Plus, last night was amazing for me, too."

I gave him a look and he laughed heartily. "I'm serious," he continued. "You have no idea what it did to me to see you falling apart underneath me."

"I just want you now," I whined. Jesus, when had I become such a wanton woman?

"Come over tonight," he said. "And I'll live up to my promise."

I smiled up at him and wondered just how bold I could be. Maintaining eye contact with him, I snaked my hand down his body and took a grasp of his hardening dick. His moans encouraged the move. I marveled at the feeling of his dick in my hand. It was simultaneously hard and soft, with a certain weight to it. I found it so arousing and so intimidating. I moved my hand over it lightly a few times, mimicking what I'd seen of hand jobs in porn, but I blushed at my inexperience. Was he even enjoying it?

If I was creative about it, maybe I could turn it into a sexy thing. He seemed to like me talking to him last night, communicating with him. I may not have known exactly what I was doing, but I could turn it into an opportunity to turn him on.

I looked up at him shyly and took a deep breath. "I ... uh ..." I began. "Sh-Show me how you like it?"

Austin let out a shuddering breath and looked at me with hooded eyes. He snaked his hand down our wet bodies to accompany mine on his dick, showing me the rhythm.

"Yes," he moaned out. "Just like that. Squeeze tighter ... God, yes."

My confidence swelled and after a few strokes, his hand fell away to grip my hip. My eyes darted between his bliss-flushed face and my hand moving over his dick. His face was nothing like I'd ever seen before. The expression was so open, so incredible that I found myself completely entranced by it.

Austin reached his hand down again to cup his hand over me and start feeling my crotch. My clit was burning to be touched, but I gently pushed his hand away. He looked into my eyes in confusion.

"Last night was all about me. Today is all about you," I explained.

Austin swallowed thickly. "You really don't need to do that."

"I know," I answered. "I want to."

And just like that, without thinking, I was on my knees before him on the floor of the shower. He barely had a moment to stare at me with wide eyes when I slowly stuck my tongue out and used it to lick the very tip of his cock. I couldn't tell you what possessed me to do it, but it must have been some combination of my own arousal, my desire to pleasure Austin, and secretly, my own need to know what this new part of him tasted like. Austin's whole body reacted, shaking, as the sounds of his moans filled the room.

"God, Hannah," he moaned. "That's incredible."

I proceeded to continue with a few experimental licks, running my tongue over different parts of him to see what would get me a groan, what would earn me a whisper of my name, and what would cause him to hold his breath and then release it in a massive sigh. I didn't mind the taste of him. He tasted like clean skin and smelled like his intoxicating body wash. If anything, I liked it because it reminded me so much of him.

It seemed to me that Austin liked it when I played with the very tip of him, especially short, fluttery stroked of my tongue over his slit. I cautiously sucked the head of his dick into my mouth, slowly experimenting with the new sensations overwhelming me. I could feel him swelling in my mouth as he moaned above me. I sucked him instinctively, as if I were sucking a lollipop. He seemed to enjoy the suction and the pressure. I pressed my tongue to the underside of his head, just at the ridge. A sigh of "fuck" slipped past his lips.

I needed him to come and wanted to see just how far I could go. I dropped my jaw and tried to take him in deeper, mimicking the motions of my hands from earlier with my mouth. Austin seemed to really be getting into it, but hissed in pain. I froze and looked up in alarm, feeling my stomach drop. I'd done what I had feared: something wrong. But Austin's aroused face was tender, and he gently stroked the side of my face in encouragement.

"Your teeth," he explained. "Can be amazing in some circumstances. Just not down there."

I withdrew him from my mouth and laughed softly. He smiled down at me. That's something that I'd come to appreciate about Austin. No matter how intense things started to feel for me, Austin was always able to cut the tension and relax me with a small affectionate comment or a little, well-timed joke. He was always reminding me that it was just me and it was just him. When things got awkward, when mistakes happened, we could take it in stride because we were us and we cared about each other. We can figure this out. I really loved that about him.

Love? Where did that come from? A shadow passed over me briefly. I realized we still hadn't talked about what any of this meant ... As hot as all of it was, the last time we'd talked about the two of us together, we had resolved to set aside our attraction to each other and try to maintain a normal teacher to student relationship. We had both clearly decided to buck this decision, but what did it mean? Were we together now? Or just fucking? Did he want that? How would us seeing each other even work? I still had another half a semester to go. And then, even if we were together, it would still be pretty taboo for him to be seeing a former student of his. Would he want to risk his reputation and go there with me? He had seized me last night in passion in the middle of his darkened living room. We hadn't thought this out. Was any of this even the right decision?

"Hey," Austin said softly. "Are you okay?"

I looked up at him. He would stop this, all of this, if I asked him to. I knew he would. At my word, all of this would come to an end. But I didn't want this to end. Did I want a relationship with him? Well ... that's something I'd have to think about. But I knew that I wanted him. I wanted him to be the one to take me all the way there. Wasn't all of this what I'd always wanted? The passion, the heat, the wonder that made me forget where I was and what I was doing. Austin made me feel that abandon. I felt it towards him constantly, even when quietly making Danny mac and cheese while he sat at the table, marking up papers.

And I felt tender toward him, too. I felt a yearning for him when I saw the way he interacted with his son, when he got that intense look of concentration while organizing a lecture, when I spied that red marker in his back pocket every time he turned to do something. I liked him and I liked being around him. Our situation was never ideal, but I felt comfortable around him. Whether it was just sex or just for tonight, I wanted him. And I could be okay with that.

In response to his question, I maintained eye contact, watching his expression and entreating him to see what I was doing to him. I folded my lips over my teeth and began to slowly take him into my mouth, as deep as I could manage.

Austin's hand was on me again, but this time not to stop me. He stroked my face, framing it and guiding my mouth gently as we stared into each other's eyes. It felt like the most intense and intimate thing I'd ever done.

I could sense that he was nearing his peak, but wasn't quite there yet. I increased my suction and Austin responded with a deep moan. "God, that feels incredible," he panted out. Experimentally, I reached up my other hand and gingerly cupped his balls. I didn't know if he would like it, but the sensitive organ begged to be touched. I softly massaged them in my hand, knowing of their sensitivity and adjusting accordingly.

Austin's breath sped up. "Shit, you're going to make me come, baby," he panted. "I'm close."

He lightly pulled on the back of my head, trying to warn me of his orgasm, but I was determined to see this to the end. I sucked on him firmly, drawing him fully into my mouth, staring up at him to watch his orgasm. And then it was happening. Austin's entire body stiffened. His face became slack as a moan that seemed to begin at the base of his spine was released from his mouth.

His dick became even more engorged, the height of its size, and his come began to run out over the back of my tongue in a series of successive spurts. I eagerly swallowed it down, barely tasting its sweet and sour flavor. I didn't know how much a man was supposed to come, but it seemed like a lot to me.

Once he finally finished, he began to soften in my mouth, gasping with sensitivity as I withdrew it. It was barely a second from the moment I withdrew him from my mouth to when he was pulling me up into a standing position and pressing my back to his chest, his groin to my ass. My knees protested in cramped pain, but that thought faded away as Austin reached his hand down to test my wetness.

"You're soaking," Austin breathed into my neck. "That turned you on, didn't it? You liked making love to me with your mouth..."

Unceremoniously, Austin entered me with his two central fingers, vigorously fucking me with the heel of his hand brutally rubbing against my clit. I began to scream out in surprise and relief when Austin's other hand clapped over my mouth.

"Shh, baby."

This was not what I had gotten last night. This was not the tender, slow introduction to penetration. This was a relentless fucking, seeking my orgasm expressly. And within a few minutes, I was coming so hard I saw spots, shouting against Austin's hand, my whole body shaking and shuddering against his. I struggled to catch my breath as Austin turned off the now cold water pouring down our bodies. With the muffling sound of the water gone, the sound of our heated breathing filled the small echoing bathroom. After a moment standing there, completely soaked, gripping each other for dear life, Austin spoke.

"I've never come that hard in my life," he said with a shallow, breathless laugh.

"Yeah, I think I may have gone blind with that one," I responded.

Austin planted one last kiss to the back of my head before exiting the shower. He went to the small cabinet under his sink and opened it, pulling out two plush white towels. He dropped one on the sink and returned to the shower, opening the door and holding out a hand for me. I eagerly took it as he helped me step out onto the bath mat. He began rubbing down my body, drying me. Once he was satisfied, he wrapped me in the towel then reached for his own, unceremoniously brushing himself down.

Once we left the bathroom, I looked at my clothing piled on his dresser and blushed. I desperately wanted to go home, eat breakfast, and prepare for the night. I turned to him, with my mouth open to say an excuse, when I was interrupted by a stomping noise down the hall.

"Sounds like Danny's up," Austin said as he pulled on his jeans. "Wait here and I'll get him settled."

I nodded and Austin pulled on a shirt and hurried out of the room. I was filled with guilt. Danny. I hadn't even thought about him once and I was supposed to be one of his caretakers. While doing my thinking in the shower earlier, he hadn't even crossed my mind. Did he know I was here? Wouldn't that be confusing for him?

I awkwardly began pulling on last night's clothes. I'd never done a walk of shame before, but now I understood why it felt so crappy. Though I was well-rested, I badly needed to change my clothes and take a proper shower. I was doing a final sweep of my things in the room when Austin returned.

"Okay, he's got his iPad with his cartoons on so he's set for about another hour, if you want to slip out of here," he said.

"Yeah, I should head out," I said reluctantly.

"Of course," he responded lightly. He drew me into his chest and kissed me deeply, my first since I'd stepped into the shower this morning. I realized that I had begun to miss his kisses, even when it had only been a few minutes between them. After a moment, he pulled away and rested his forehead against mine.

"I know it might be a little late to be having this conversation, but I want you to know without a doubt that I've been tested and I'm completely clean of all STDs," he said.

Protection. That was another thing I hadn't even thought about, or had forgotten about the instant his lips touched mine. Not that I thought he had anything, but it did put me a little at ease to know that.

"As you know, I've never been with anyone else. And I've never done anything like this, even," I said. I licked my lips. "And ... and I'm on the Pill."

The thickness in the air returned between us.

"Will I see you tonight?" he asked hopefully.

"What time?"

"Come over around seven."

"I'll be here."

CHAPTER NINE

"You should see your face when you talk about her," Leo said, over a mouthful of sandwich. After I'd told him about everything that went down with Hannah last night, he was looking at me more seriously than I think I'd ever seen him. "You're starting to have feelings for her."

I stared down at my sandwich in frustration. I'd completely lost my appetite. "Is that so bad? She's smart, kind, great with Danny, fucking ... fucking *amazing* to touch. Why wouldn't I care for her?"

"'Care' isn't the word I would use," Leo cautioned. "The Austin I know wouldn't risk his career and his reputation on a woman surrounded by such baggage. You feel more for her than that."

I had no time to respond, because before I knew it, a young, red-haired woman was stomping up to our table, looking pissed off. She planted her salad onto the table in front of her. "Are you Dr. Austin Parks?" she asked.

"Yeah," I responded cautiously.

"I'm Annie Owens," she responded. "I'm Hannah's best

friend. You may recognize me from the club the other night. Or maybe not. You were a tad ... preoccupied."

I could feel the color drain my face. What did she know? What had Hannah told her? From the look on her face, it seemed that the answer to both of those questions was everything. A tense moment passed, where both of us waited for the other to make the next move. Leo cleared his throat uncomfortably.

"Hi," he said. "I'm Professor Leo Gill. And I know everything about Austin and Hannah."

We both turned our heads to him sharply. "What?" he asked. "I do! Clearly, neither Austin nor Hannah can keep anything from their best friends."

"No one asked you," Annie snapped.

Leo whistled. "Meow," he said, before leaning down to slurp up some of his soda.

Annie rolled her eyes and turned her attention back to me. "I just want you to know that I know everything that's going on with Hannah. And if you hurt her, I will end you."

"Whoa!" Leo exclaimed.

"Wait a minute, hang on," I interjected. "I'm not going to hurt her. I'm afraid of what impression of me she's given, if you think that."

"I don't know you, or a thing about you. But Hannah is a very special person."

"I know."

"And she likes you a lot."

"I like her, too—"

"And you need to know that she has me in her corner if you try to do anything funny."

Leo jumped in. "A fighter. I like that."

"I said, buzz off," Annie retorted.

I could feel my rage rise inside of me. Who the hell did this girl think she was? I was about to tell her to fuck right off, when she began speaking in a softer voice.

"Imagine you were me," she reasoned. "What would this situation look like to you? Your best friend having a good time with a guy, or a professor taking advantage of a student, with so much at stake. Her dignity, her grades, possibly the rest of her life. She needs to graduate next month, not worry about what your sorry ass is doing. How am I supposed to know you're not a predator, that this isn't a pattern of behavior that you've had before? Hannah trusts you. I don't. And I shouldn't."

I took a deep breath, centering myself before I responded. "I don't just like Hannah," I began. "I respect her. I would never do anything that she hadn't asked me to do first. And, of course I know what's at stake. I have my own career on the line. I have a young son, who I love and need to support myself. This isn't a pattern of behavior. Nothing like this has ever happened to me before. And I'm trying to be careful here, but that'd be much easier to do if I didn't have you accosting me in such a public place."

Annie raised her chin petulantly. "You may be telling the truth. And I really hope you are. But you need to know that I know about this and won't let you get away with it if you're lying."

With that, she picked up her plate and strutted away.

I ENTERED my office and stopped in my tracks when I saw the dean of my school, Harry Arthur, scrutinizing one of my bookshelves.

"Dean Arthur," I said, trying to sound official.

"Oh, Austin, I told you to call me Harry," he responded. "I hope you don't mind that I let myself in. Did I interrupt your lunch?"

I looked down at my half-eaten, haphazardly wrapped sandwich and tried to put it back in my bag discreetly. "No, not at all," I assured him. "Please, have a seat."

I took my place in my chair as Harry casually perched himself on the arm of one of my other chairs. "I was just admiring your books. It's quite a collection," he continued.

"Thank you, sir," I said, trying to stifle the confusion in my voice. "To what do I owe the honor of this visit?"

"So formal, always," Harry smiled. "I wanted to ask you about Hannah Cosgrove."

I could feel my heart drop into my stomach and I struggled to tamp it down and keep my face unaffected. I had no clue what he knew. I couldn't jump to conclusions.

"Yes, she's in one of my intro classes," I said as evenly as I could. "Victorian-Era Poetry and Literature. What about her?"

"Well, what are your thoughts ... your impressions of her as a person? Competent? Hard-working?"

My heart rate calmed slightly. He didn't seem to know anything about our relationship. Was this really a purely academic question?

"Has she done something wrong?"

Harry laughed. "Quite the opposite, actually. She's on the Dean's List ... Well, *my* list, I guess. Though that feels very odd to say. Her marks are extremely high. And I'm considering her for a TA position upon graduation, if she'd be up for it. You've proven yourself to be a good professor and a good judge of character, so I was wondering what you thought of her."

I felt my heart swell at the thought of Hannah working in the same school as me, staying in the same city after graduating. I knew she wanted to be a journalist, but perhaps a TA position would be a good consistent and interesting job while she wrote and got on her feet after college. I cleared my throat.

"She's very dedicated," I elaborated, still attempting not to give anything away. "She was struggling with some of our oral assignments early on in the semester, but she persevered. She's bright and eager to learn and certainly doesn't back down from a challenge. She's really a very unique person." I clamped my mouth shut, trying to limit my words. I could honestly go on about Hannah for hours, but I needed to be careful.

"You seem to know her personally," Harry pried.

"I've also hired her as a part-time babysitter for my son," I explained, hoping that would be sufficient.

"Ah, I see. So you're biased," Harry joked, his aging eyes twinkling.

I laughed lightly. "I suppose I am."

Something flashed in Harry's eyes, something knowing. I fought to calm my features again and look like less of a dopey idiot.

"Do you usually get personally involved with students?"

The question was shocking and too on-the-nose. "I try not to."

"But she's an exception."

"There's kind of an awkward story to that," I coughed out. "You see, she and I had already met before she enrolled in my class and neither of us knew we were professor and student."

"Isn't that interesting," Harry suggested. "What about you, Austin? What are your aspirations?"

I tried to surreptitiously wipe my sweaty palms on my slacks. "I love teaching. My son is settled here in the city. I'd like to raise him up as best as I can, keep working here, maybe do some research. I think I'd like to write a book at some point."

"And you're the kind of person that would prioritize your family and your work?"

Oh, Jesus. Did he know? "Of course, sir."

Harry looked down at his hands momentarily, then back up at me. "Good. I'm glad we understand each other." He rose and made a motion to leave, until thinking of something and turning back to me.

"How about this," he began. "I have a few other candidates I'm considering in liberal arts, but Hannah's record puts her pretty high on the list. If I select her, I'll let you tell her the good news."

"Whatever works best for you," I gushed.

"Of course. Well, have a good evening, Austin."

With that he left, closing the door quietly behind him.

CHAPTER TEN

I reached my hand up to knock on Austin's door for the third time before thinking better. *This is stupid,* I thought to myself. *I have a key; shouldn't I just let myself in?* And in any other case I would have, without a second thought. But tonight was different. Tonight gave me pause.

I almost clawed Annie's eyes out of her sockets when she came back to the apartment, grinning like a cat that caught the biggest and fattest mouse of all. When I finally asked her why, she told me that she had given Austin "the business" about our "arrangement." I felt absolutely mortified and texted Austin to apologize to him instantly. Luckily, he took it in stride and responded that he was still ready for tonight if I was.

And, of course, I was. So I had no idea why I was so nervous at all. Austin and I had already been naked together, done almost everything together. Was going all the way really that much different? I still had questions about the status of our relationship. I still wanted to know what was about to happen between us, what the consequences might be. But I had never let myself throw caution to the wind like this before. I had never opened myself up to the world, to indecision, to not knowing what came next.

I decided to just open the door. I was being too awkward. What would sex goddess Hannah do? She would take the bull by the horns and walk on in there without a thought. I tested the door and found it unlocked. My eyes widened to see what awaited me in the foyer. Several flameless candles sat on the floor, trailing down the small hallway and up the staircase. In the unlit room, the effect was dreamy, ethereal, and romantic.

I grinned and followed the path of lights up the stairs and down the hall to Austin's room. His room was decorated in much the same way. All the lights were off, but the flameless candles covered nearly every available surface in the room, creating a soothing, flickering glow. Austin was sitting in a comfortable-looking chair, facing the window, which cast planes of moonlight across the room.

He looked up when I entered and smiled, checking his watch. "You're so prompt."

"I'm a timely gal. Am I interrupting your work?"

He closed his book and rose from his seat. In a few strides, he was holding me and kissing me gently on the mouth. When the kiss ended, he spoke. "I don't usually fill my house with candles for ambience. You know I was waiting for you."

"Well, who am I to judge your process?" I teased.

"Are you hungry at all?" he asked. "I have some food, if you'd like."

"Maybe later," I replied. "I think I might be a bit too nervous to eat."

"There's no reason to be nervous. It's just me," he comforted.

"Where's Danny?" I asked curiously.

"Sleeping over with a friend," he explained. "So ... you don't have to be quiet tonight."

I swallowed, my throat suddenly dry. Austin stroked the side of my face reassuringly. "Are you sure about this?" he asked, for what felt like the hundredth time. It was really starting to annoy me, but I reminded myself that he was trying to look out for me. As far as I knew, he'd never even been with a virgin before. But who was I to project or assume... All I knew was that he was just as nervous and keyed up as I was.

"I'm sure," I said.

But I was stuck in my head, overthinking it again. This time, when Austin kissed me, he was fighting my nerves and I could feel myself getting tense. Sensing this, he stopped kissing me and rested his forehead against mine, running his hands all over my body.

"Do you know what I find sexiest about you?"

I smiled up at him, shaking my head.

"Well, firstly, your body is amazing. The way you move it is amazing. From the moment I saw you dancing in the club that first day we met, there was no way I wasn't going to be absolutely magnetized to you." He gripped my hips, swaying us slightly in a broken dance. I could already feel the tension begin to fall off of me.

"You're an incredibly open person," he continued. "And you're not intimidated by me, by a hard assignment, by life. You barely even flinch."

He didn't usually talk to me like this. I should've stopped him, but I couldn't. These words were rare and beautiful and I had to hear them.

"But if I had to pick one thing, one single thing above all others as what I find sexiest about you, it would have to be your incredible persistence and dedication to something that you care about or want to do. You always go that extra mile with your work or while taking care of Danny."

Bizarrely, I could feel tears fill my eyes and a lump form in my throat. I was floored by my emotional reaction to his words and intimidated by the power of them. I couldn't take any more. Blinking back my tears, I pressed forward and joined my lips with his. This time, the kiss didn't skip a beat. We were fully there, taken with each other as we had been on all other kisses before. I poured everything into the kiss, trying to tell him that I was thankful for him, that I wanted him, that I was ready.

Breaking the kiss, I took a half step back from him, creating some scant space between us. He watched me raptly as I slowly, *slowly* began to remove my clothes. I'd opted for a button-down shirt tucked into a high-waisted long black skirt. A little bit formal for heading to a sexual tryst, I'm sure, but I wanted to feel comfortable and I wanted to feel confident. Perhaps there was a sex fiend inside of me that would get on the subway in a sheer shirt and wear no underwear, but that day was a bit beyond me at this point.

I untucked my shirt and watched his face as my hands moved further and further down. Once completely unbuttoned, I shrugged the shirt off, trying to maintain my aura of sexuality. The skirt was a quick work, pooling at my feet with a swift un-zip. I heard Austin's swift intake of breath, saw his pupils dilating, and I knew I'd made the right choice with the lingerie. After cycling through my options, I had sheepishly knocked on Annie's door, assuring her I was still mad at her, but I needed her help. It took her less than a few moments to respond.

"Black lace," she said decisively. "You can never go wrong with black lace."

Austin was now staring at me as if he were a hungry man trying to figure out where to start with a Thanksgiving feast. I couldn't help but smirk to myself. I reached up and back to unhook the closure of my bra, but then Austin was there in front of me, stopping my hands.

"Please let me do at least some of it," he begged. His voice rasped out desperately. I was enjoying the fact that he seemed more worked up than I was.

"All right," I conceded. "Besides, you're overdressed now."

I reached forward and made a game of slowly unbuttoning his own shirt. I touched him with a new confidence, no longer fretting over whether or not I was doing something right. Instead, I let myself indulge in him. He'd showered recently and he smelled like an intoxicating mix of his body wash, skin, and a completely-unique-to-him manly musk. Once the shirt was completely removed, I leaned my face into his chest, inhaling deeply and pressing my lips above his increasing heartbeat.

Austin was having his own preoccupations with me. He wasn't satisfied to simply let me undress him. He was touching me all over, kissing my shoulders and neck, leaning down to trace up my jaw and capture my earlobe between his lips, tugging it into his mouth. I moaned aloud. I'd never had my ear kissed before and I strangely found that I loved the sensation.

"You're distracting me," I attempted to scold him.

"Me? You're the distracting one," he heatedly murmured into the nape of my neck.

I reached down to undo his belt, shucking it quickly and dropping it to the floor with a clank. I worked his button open and unzipped his fly, easing his pants over his ass and down to the floor. His boxer briefs shaped alluringly to his ass and the tops of his muscular thighs. The clasp closures at the front were straining to accommodate his already engorged cock. I smiled. I felt like I understood the language of his body already. Reading him came second nature to me.

"Already so excited?" I teased.

In response, he ran his hands down my back and over my bare ass cheeks, spreading them slightly. He slid his hand underneath the fabric of my thong and traced my crack from back to front, feeling my collecting wetness. I gasped in response.

"Seems like you are, too," he said.

I boldly undid the clasps on his briefs, pulling his dick out and stroking it. He moaned against me.

"Ah, fuck," he murmured. "I can't get enough of you."

Austin's hands moved back up and around my ass to grip my hips. In a few awkward steps, he backed me up to the edge of the bed, where I was able to slightly recline. He brought one knee up onto the bed and left a foot on the floor, with me still stroking him. From the slightly more distant and lower position, he craned his head down to pepper kisses on my breasts. He found his way to my erect nipples, sucking them through my lacy bra. The combination of his mouth and the slightly scratchy texture of my bra pulled moans from my mouth, and I could feel an accompanying gush of arousal in my pussy. I started stroking him faster, with more enthusiasm.

I was concentrating so hard on my work and his ministrations that I barely felt his hands come back up and undo the clasp of my bra. I stopped massaging his dick to pull off the bra completely, and as soon as the article was gone, we were right back on each other. We kissed again, briefly but passionately, and instantly returned to the work of tending to each other's pleasure. His attention to my breasts was so thorough I was sure they would be covered in hickeys in the morning.

"Stop sucking so hard," I barely got out in my already ruined voice. "You're going to give me hickeys."

"Does that bother you?" he asked. "You seem to be really enjoying it." To make his point, he sucked one of my breasts into his mouth, feeling me shudder underneath him in pleasure. He released me with a pop. "Do you really want me to stop?" He repeated the action to the other breast and I cried out, holding his head to my chest. I could feel him shake with laughter. "I thought so."

He continued to torture me while I continued to play with him. We followed each other's rhythms: him sucking and kissing me in time with my strokes to him and vice versa. The fact that we were fully in sync was almost as arousing as the actual physical sensations. After a few moments passed, Austin yanked my hand away from him suddenly.

"Stop," he panted. "Stop. If you keep going, I'm going to explode all over the place."

I could feel myself grinning. He smiled back at me. "What're you grinning at?" he asked.

"I don't know ... I like that I get you so worked up," I bragged. He laughed in response.

"You honestly have no idea what you do to me." He reached down and pulled down my underwear, bearing me fully to him. "And what that makes me want to do to you."

"Yes," I hissed as he reached down and began stroking my outer lips. He scooted my body up the bed, moving me as if I weighed nothing, finally joining me on the bed completely, but staying close to my crotch, scrutinizing my reactions. I moaned out. "Please."

His eyes flashed as he looked up at me. "You liked this, didn't you? You like my mouth on your pussy."

I moaned. "God, yes, please."

He groaned in response. "I love how responsive you're being," he said as he leaned his face down to my crotch. He took a quick lap of me, causing me to gasp. "And I love how you taste."

There was that word again. Love. I felt myself freeze for a moment, about to go into another fit of overthinking. But Austin had other plans. He didn't give me enough time to go on that tear. In the next moment, his mouth was on me, driving me home. I reached down and grabbed fists of his hair, thinking only distantly of avoiding hurting him. He didn't seem bothered in the least. His tongue painted an alluring picture all over me, both of us covered in my releases and his saliva. He began to ease two fingers inside of me. I could feel him scissoring them, spreading me open.

The sensation was strange but made me feel fuller, already so ready to receive him. My mind began to run away from me. I moved my hips against his face, using his tongue for my pleasure while I fantasized about his cock finally being joined with me. It was intoxicating, empowering, and felt so goddamn amazing. Already so worked up, I could feel myself nearing my peak. He felt it too and began the stiff, small strokes over my clit with the tip of his tongue that he knew would finish me. He held me to the bed as I finished, gasping for air, my arms falling uselessly to the bed.

"God," he panted against my inner thigh. "I need to be inside you. Can I be inside you?"

"Finally. Please!" He laughed to himself and I could feel myself blush. "Don't laugh at me," I scolded. "I've been waiting for this for a long time, Austin."

He reached forward and stroked my face, staring into my eyes. "I'll make it worth the long wait, baby. I promise."

I felt that thickness in my chest again. I was so discomfited by the new sensation, but being here with him, I somehow sensed that he was feeling the same thing. I turned my head to kiss the palm of his hand. "Show me," I said.

He sat back on his knees, pulling off his boxer briefs. Had they seriously stayed on that whole time? His cock sprang forward and unable to help myself, I turned suddenly, crawling forward onto my stomach to pull it into my mouth, licking up the bead of pre-cum that had accumulated at his tip and sucking on him firmly.

"Oh, Hannah," he breathed. "Go easy, baby, or I won't be able to last. That's incredible. You're incredible," he said.

He leaned across the bed and opened the top drawer of his bedside dresser. He withdrew with a small bottle of lube. I looked at him questioningly as he squeezed some out onto his hand and began to coat his dick with it.

"Are you seriously concerned I'm not wet enough?" I asked him.

He laughed. "Don't get me wrong. I love that you're sopping, but you can never be too wet."

I laid back again and looked at him purposefully as I reached down and stroked my hand over my face-fucked pussy. I collected some of the wetness in my palm and reached forward, spreading it over the head of his dick and stroking it down. He twitched as he watched me rub myself all over him. When I released him and leaned back, his dick was fully hard and he was panting. He almost looked close to orgasm.

"That's the craziest and hottest thing I've ever seen," he breathed. "I'm fucking ... I'm seeing spots right now."

"Take your time," I purred, feeling very satisfied with myself.

He leaned down and laid over me, our whole naked bodies touching from head to foot. He kissed me leisurely, as if we had all the time in the world. Finally, he released me. "Don't worry," he assured me. "I fully intend to."

He aligned his hips with mine and embraced me with another kiss. I moaned at the sensation of contact between his hot, slippery cock and my sensitive folds. *This is it,* I thought. *This is happening.* But instead of entering me, Austin did something I didn't expect. Looping his arms around my shoulders, he rolled us both onto our sides, facing each other. He propped himself up slightly with the arm underneath him to avoid crushing my leg beneath his hips. With his other arm, he swung my opposite leg up and over his hip, pulling us flush together.

Holding the back of my ass firmly against him, he started grinding against me, his cock sliding through my lips again and again. I moaned and started rocking against him, too. Austin leaned his head down then and pulled one of my sensitive peaks into his mouth, sucking like he knew I liked. I could feel myself gush again, dripping all over myself and his dick. The sensation was amazing and like nothing I'd ever experienced before, but still wasn't enough. I needed him inside.

"Please," I begged. "I'm ready."

Austin looked into my eyes, trying to make sure I was being completely serious, before reaching his hand down and taking hold of himself. He lined himself up to me and I could feel myself clenching in anticipation. He paused to rub the head against my clit, teasing both of us with the most sensitive parts.

"Relax," he murmured. "If you're relaxed, it'll feel much better."

I nodded and took a deep breath, focusing on the sensations of our skin brushing, the pleasure and openness still present in my pelvic floor, and I felt myself relaxing and loosening. Austin must have sensed the change too, because he realigned himself with me. After a few moments, he began to slowly push in.

When I felt his head first penetrate me, I knew that this would be completely different from his fingers. He was smooth, impossibly hot, and the sensation was completely novel and arousing. He didn't fully enter me, to my dismay. He continued his small thrusts just at my entrance, going agonizingly slowly.

The motion worked me open and into a frenzy. Gradually, he began to enter me further and further with each thrust. I was panting, completely overtaken by the feeling. But I still felt empty. I needed to be fully joined with him. I wrapped my leg firmly around him and tried to push him in completely.

"Please," I begged again. "I need all of you."

He growled low in his throat and sure enough, his next

thrust buried him to the hilt, our hips flush together. I moaned deeply. To my surprise and delight, I felt no pain, just the faraway pressure of his girth inside of me. I could feel his heartbeat, hammering against me through his chest, and I could feel it pulsing in his dick inside of me. I tipped my head up to stare at him. I found him looking down at me, a sincere and cryptic look on his face. I watched his throat bob as he swallowed.

He gripped my ass again and I reached forward to grab his shoulders as he began moving again. This was so different than I had thought it would be. I had expected the pain of his entry, classic missionary position, and lying back while he fucked me. I couldn't help but think that this position was a very deliberate choice. He didn't want to just fuck me. He wanted us to be able to fuck each other, something this side-by-side position was made for.

He still hadn't ceased his eye contact with me. My hips began to move in time with his, feeling and matching his rhythm. He picked up the pace, moving in and out of me as we both started panting. His eyes bored into mine as we both began to climb the peak. As my hips were fully fucking him back, he released my ass and his hand came up to my face to cradle it as our hips snapped together. His mouth fell open as his breath came out harsher. I leaned forward to lightly bite his swollen lower lip and he groaned, speeding up again as I pulled it into my mouth.

"Are you close?" he gasped out.

"Almost," I groaned. I squeezed my eyes shut, concentrating on my orgasm. Austin let go of my face and stretched his hand down between us to rub my clit furiously. I cried out.

"Open your eyes," he demanded. "Open your eyes. I want to see you come."

I struggled to blink my eyes open to see him biting his lip, eagerly trying to finish me. In one, two, three more strokes, I gasped.

"Oh, God, I'm coming! Austin!" My mouth fell open in a silent cry as tremors and waves began to rock for me, my pussy fluttering around his dick.

"Fuck, oh, fuck," he muttered. And I could feel him release inside of me, warmth flooding me as we both collapsed, panting and moaning to each other in the afterglow.

Austin's body lay prone against mine, the full weight of his arm and heavily muscled thighs pinning me to the bed. I liked the pressure of his body on mine. The weight held me to my spot on the bed, but also held me in the glorious moment of post-coital bliss. I still couldn't feel the encroaching creeping of sanity or thought. I was still somewhere on a cloud.

"I'm trying so hard not to crush you," he panted against my clavicle. "But that was the most intense thing I've ever experienced."

I stretched out my toes to flex the bottoms of my legs. My own calves were tight from my curling toes. I sighed as Austin sat up, peppering the tops of my breasts with small kisses. "That was ... I mean ..."

Austin smirked to himself. "A journalist lost for words? Should I be flattered or very worried?"

I grinned and guided his face to mine, pulling him into a kiss. "It was perfect. Thank you." He smiled and kissed me back. I couldn't believe how hungry we still were for each other. Even after we had pushed each other to release, the kiss still felt wonderful and new. It took no time at all for it to develop into a deep and passionate kiss and, almost instinctually, our hips started rocking together again. Austin broke the kiss with a gasp.

"If you're not feeling too sore, we can go again." He said the statement more as a question, the whole time lightly thrusting into me, still tightly encased inside of me.

"Seriously?" I asked. "I thought it usually took a long time between when a guy comes and when he can be hard again."

"It usually does. But something about you ... I haven't been able to do this since I was a teenager."

I wrinkled my nose. "Am I supposed to take that as a compliment?"

He shrugged. "I didn't mean it as one. What I mean is ... I'm not getting any younger here, but being with you makes me feel brand new. And considering it's never happened before, or at least since that time, I can't help but attribute at least some of it to you."

"Well, I will go ahead and take that one as a compliment. So, thank you." Austin planted a kiss to the center of my forehead and grasped my hips. I could feel myself jolt with desire at the prospect of having him again, but he framed my hips and slowly pulled himself out with a hiss. My whole body responded to the withdrawal.

"No," I gasped, gripping his forearms and trying to scoot myself closer to him. "Why are you leaving?" Austin gently rolled me onto my back and kissed me, soothing my panic.

"You didn't say anything to my offer. It's okay to be sore."

I tuned into my body for a moment, searching for signs of tenderness or soreness anywhere. All I could feel was the abundant wetness inside of me, the beating of my heart, and the peaking of my arousal as I yet again admired the form of his magnificent body.

"I'm not sore," I panted, reaching down to stroke his dick. He moaned at the contact. My motions were eased by our commingling. His skin was soaked and I could only imagine at the state my pussy was in. I could feel his semi-hard dick becoming a full-blown hard-on in my hand and was thrilled and emboldened by the feeling. "You made it so good for me."

"You're just not feeling it now," he assured me through

gritted teeth. "My dick is much thicker than my fingers. You've been stretched a lot today."

I rolled my eyes and tightened my grip around him. "Try not to sound so proud when you say that next time. It's made to be stretched, isn't it?"

His hands tightened on the sheets next to my shoulders. He appeared already too gone to respond before he swallowed roughly. "If you say so ..."

He gingerly removed my hand from him, leaning back to kneel on his heels. "I'd like to do something I think you'll enjoy."

I nodded and smirked as I watched him. He leaned away, staring at my body, spread and ready, lying before him.

"Touch yourself," he demanded.

My heart skipped a beat. "W-What?" I asked him, although I'd heard exactly what he said. I could feel a blush begin at my chest and crawl up my neck, curling around my ears.

"I want to see you pleasure yourself," he stated simply. "I want to watch what you like."

"You know what I like."

"Please? Think of me and ... pretend I'm not even here."

I gulped. "I ... I'll try ..." I began to reach my shaking hand down the front of my body, Austin's wide eyes following me the whole way. I couldn't stand the look on his face, so I allowed my eyes to close, concentrating on my pleasure and feeling the rest of the world float away.

Slowly, I began by making leisurely circles around my clit. I thrilled at the sensitivity and the wetness, more present than whenever I did this alone. I exhaled on a moan, feeling my muscles already begin to tense, ready to chase my orgasm. Losing myself to the sensations, I slowly slipped a finger inside of myself, feeling my walls flutter. The whole time, I was thinking of Austin. The things he did to me, how much I wanted him. My legs fidgeted as I impatiently waited for him, wishing he'd stop this and just take me already. I exhaled his name on a turned-on sigh.

"Austin," I groaned.

"Oh, fuck."

My eyes snapped open and there was the object of my desire in front of me. Breathing, in the flesh, Austin sat facing me, watching me with hooded eyes and stroking himself slowly. I had almost forgotten that I had the real thing in front of me, to touch, to fuck, to eat up with my eyes.

Suddenly, Austin leaned forward, releasing himself. He grasped the hand I was using to pleasure myself. I moaned in protest but his eyes were mad, begging me. He was asking me not to deny him, but he wasn't demanding. I let him gently pull my hand, withdrawing my finger from myself. Slowly, he lifted my hand up to his lips and licked my own liquids off my finger, maintaining eye contact the whole time. He released my finger with a pop, grinning at me impishly.

"Couldn't help myself," he said, readjusting himself and sitting back on his knees. My stomach bottomed out as I thrilled at the thought of him entering me again.

Austin widened his legs a little bit, his already-leaking dick pointing directly at me. He slung both of my legs over his, spreading me for him. "Missionary. How traditional," I commented.

His eyes flashed as he glanced up at me from his work. "Not exactly," he responded cryptically. I raised an eyebrow in questioning. Austin reached up to the head of the bed and plucked one of the unused pillows. Before I could ask what it was for, he looped an arm under the crooks of each of my knees, pulling upward and raising my hips off the bed. He slid the pillow under me and scooted a little bit closer, trying to get just the right position. He put my legs back in their places, draped over his thighs. We were in sort of an open missionary position, with his body upright, my upper body horizontal against the bed, and my hips angled up towards his at a forty-degree angle.

"You're so far away," I whined as he took himself in one hand and began to rub my lips and clit with the other. The complaint left my mind as I moaned in response.

"All in good time, Hannah. God, I love you like this," he sighed. "You're dripping. And I can't tell where I end and you begin." He dipped his fingers into me experimentally and my hips automatically lifted to chase the feeling.

"You're ready," he commented in a husky voice. He withdrew his fingers then and returned his hand to his dick, lining himself up with my entrance.

I licked my lips. "Maybe ... maybe you make me want it a lot, too."

He paused and made eye contact with me, our eyes darkly pinned to each other. He let out a deep breath, as if he'd been holding it. "Missionary position is great because you get to hold each other and fuck. Ideal for lazy days, lovemaking, taking it slow," he explained. I had no idea where this sudden tutoring in the mechanics of sexual positions came from, but I couldn't deny that it was turning me on. "But I think we've done plenty of that tonight, haven't we?"

I bit my lip and nodded. He positioned himself at my entrance, teasing it by rubbing the tip of his dick against me. "Positions like this and, even better, doggy style, are often criticized for being 'less personal.' I disagree. And from this angle, I hit your G-spot every time." With that, he thrust inside of me, burying himself to the hilt. My eyes and mouth flashed open as spears of pleasure pierced every nerve in my body. I gasped for breath.

"Holy fuck!" I shouted. His hands moved to grip my thighs, holding my hips in place, his palms searing prints into the flushed flesh there. I reached my hands down to grab his wrists, desperate for him. "Please, more." I moaned.

He obliged, launching into deep, penetrating, flooring thrusts. He alternated between powerful, slow thrusts that rocked me the same way the first did, and short, shallow thrusts rubbing against that delicious spot inside of me again and again. In my sexed-up haze, the thought floated across my mind that it reminded me very much of the way he went down on me: slow, shuddering sensations contrasting perfectly with fast and frantic ones.

After a particularly incredible thrust, my eyes rolled back into my head and more words were ripped from my throat. "Austin, fuck," I moaned.

His eyes darkened. He had been watching himself enter me intently, but his head immediately snapped up at his name. Our eyes met magnetically, neither of us able to look away.

Though I liked this position *a lot,* I couldn't help but think of his comment from earlier ... That doggy style was even better. Once the thought was caught in my head, I couldn't shake it. He fucked me for a few more heated strokes and it felt so good that I almost completely lost my nerve. But I was aching all over for him and I wanted to do this. Boldly, I looked up and made eye contact with him. His mouth fell open and panted at the clear change in my mood.

Determined, I pushed his hands off of me and wriggled my hips away, releasing him. Austin's face was stricken evenly by disappointment and fear that he had hurt me. I shook my head at both and scrambled onto my hands and knees, my ass facing him.

"I want to try it like this," I breathed, barely able to get the words out. For a breathless moment, nothing happened, so I worried my lip in my teeth and craned my neck back to look at Austin. He was staring at me as if he'd never seen anything like me before. He swayed for a second, dazed, before shaking his head and reaching for me, a growl in the back of his throat.

"I don't think I'll be able to hold back if I take you like this," he warned, his hands smoothing over the curves of my ass. Excitement bolted through my spine, all the way out to the tips of my fingers and my toes.

"I don't want you to," I countered. I thought he would re-enter me just then and take me brutally like I wanted him to. But instead, another tense moment passed. I could feel his hands traveling up the length of my back, briefly squeezing my shoulders. Unexpectedly, one hand snaked up into my hair, gathering it, and yanking firmly. I gasped, my head lifting back, exposing my neck. His other hand went back to my rear to position him. Once Austin had attained a satisfactory angle, he thrust into me harshly. I cried out, my neck straining against his grip in my hair. His other hand flew to my hip, grasping me as he roughly and relentlessly pounded into me.

He was right. Each thrust seemed to rut the tip of his dick against my G-spot; a constant and intense rhythm that I was fairly certain would drive me mad. I could feel my eyes rolling up into my head with each passing moment.

"You like that?" his hoarse voice demanded.

"God, yes, Austin. I love it," I barely breathed out.

"I can tell. You're so wet and ready. It feels like I'm fucking something made for me."

We were in a trance, both so far gone, so delirious that neither of us was completely mentally present. We were reduced down from our higher selves to writhing balls of need, desperate to seek release.

"Tell me how it feels to have me inside of you," Austin begged.

"Austin—" I began to protest feebly. He silenced me with a sequence of insane thrusts, seemingly focused directly onto my

G-spot. My vision spiraled out of focus and I could only see the pillow I was white-knuckle gripping in my hands. Everything else was pointless. I almost forgot what he'd even asked from me when he spoke again.

"Tell me. Tell me how it feels."

I gulped. My mouth was dry from open-mouth panting and my tongue rasped like sandpaper against the roof of my mouth. "It feels ... it feels unlike anything I've ever felt."

"Because you've never done this before."

I nodded, fighting his tightened grasp on my hair as I did so. "You're my first."

I could feel him swell inside me. He growled and began thrusting like an animal.

"That turns you on, doesn't it?" I asked.

He closed his eyes for a moment, slowing his thrusts from feverishly paced spirals to leisurely, torturous pumps.

"You are ..." he panted. "Entirely unlike anyone I've ever met. All of this is you."

I doubted either of us could have make sense of his frenzied words, even if we'd wanted to. Nevertheless, I could feel my breath hitch at hearing them. I turned away from him, letting him fuck me into the bed, gripping the sheets, and moaning so loud that I was sure his neighbors for blocks would be knocking on the door with complaints. I could feel Austin losing his rhythm as he neared his release. He grunted as he reached his hand around, his fingers fumbling frantically over my clit. I gasped at the contact.

"I'm getting close. Come with me," he breathed into my back, bowing over me as we chased release together.

"Yes," I hissed. "Yes, right there. I'm almost there."

For a few breathless thrusts, we were almost completely silent. Then, the tension within me released and I began to shake all over. I cried out as waves of pleasure rocked through me and my arms and legs gave out. The only things supporting me were Austin's arms, his rough hands holding me upright as his own pleasure followed mine. After what seemed like an eternity of pleasure, we both came down from our highs, collapsing against the cooling sheets.

After a moment, Austin rolled to the side and pulled me onto my back, my eyes already falling closed with sleep. He laid sweet kisses across my face. When his lips finally met mine, I kissed back lazily, sloppily.

"Sorry," I apologized when he broke the kiss. "I'm pretty much passing out over here."

"Please, rest. You've had a big day."

I swatted at his smirk, only causing him to laugh and smile more. I cuddled up against his chest, ready to fall asleep, but in a moment, he spoke again.

"Thank you," he whispered.

I lifted my head to look at him. "For what?"

"For letting me be your first."

The look in his eyes answered the hairs rising at the base of my neck. I could feel that tender place inside of me cracking open again, as it had countless times that night. I couldn't speak. What could I possibly say to answer him?

Instead, I grinned and leaned down to press a light kiss against his lips. I laid my head against his chest again, listening to his steady heartbeat. I pushed my anxiety away, ignoring my rising concern as the pleasure and haziness of the evening floated away. I allowed his breathing and my encroaching exhaustion to pull me into sleep.

CHAPTER ELEVEN

Giddy. It wasn't a word I'd ever used to describe myself before, but it sure fit the bill now. Annie sat on the bed and watched me with a smirk on her face. She'd been smirking like that ever since my amazing night with Austin about a week ago, after which I'd come home floating so high I was practically bumping the disgusting dorm ceiling. And now he'd asked me over to his place for dinner, no Danny again, but also no sex. He'd told me he wanted to 'get to know me outside of bed,' which was so freaking romantic that I was willing to overlook how much I wanted him every which way. And it wasn't as though we hadn't had plenty of encounters since that first night.

I'd been a little afraid he might flip out the next day—you know, some guys do—but instead he woke me up with the most tender kiss ever and from that day forward texted and emailed and met up with me in places to hold me tight, among other things. Places like the parking deck, even though he was risking a lot by being with me out in public. Places like his office, even though he was risking a lot by being with me out in public. You get the idea. He was making it eminently clear that being with me was more important to him than laying low, and that was just so hot it left me almost a puddle.

"You're disgusting," Annie commented, lounging on the bed as she carefully striped her nails with tape to create an intricate star pattern. "Look at you. You're in luuuuurve, sunshine. Admit it."

"I'm not," I protested, hiding my head in the tiny closet and pretending I was actually still looking for an outfit even though I'd already decided on a cute pair of skinny jeans and a crop top. It wasn't overtly hot, since that wasn't, apparently, what we were after tonight, but it also wasn't sackcloth. Because, you know, a girl could dream.

"Liar, liar, lace underwear on fire," she sing-songed. "You are in so much trouble, girl. The only good thing is that he obviously feels the same way. Which is great. Because otherwise I'd have to kill him."

"Annie," I admonished. She'd told me all about her little threat session with poor Austin before we'd even done anything! "It's a miracle you don't send him running off screaming."

"A best friend has a role," she shrugged as I emerged with my chosen outfit. "Oh, come on, Hannah. You're wearing *that*?"

I hadn't told her about the no-sex thing tonight. She'd have teased me into oblivion! "We're going to Danny's baseball game," I lied. "Stilettos and a bralette won't cut it."

Thankfully, she seemed to accept that and even let me dress without more comments before she got up to help me with my hair. Annie was a wizard with the curling iron and my decidedly average mane suddenly turned into tumbling sex-goddess curls.

Okay ... I stared at myself in the mirror, reaching for a gorgeous-looking curl, only to have my hand smacked. "Let it set," Annie scolded. "Or it'll frizz."

I reluctantly withdrew my hand and wondered if Austin would have nearly the same reaction.

. . .

He did! When he opened the door at his place and took one look at me, it was the first time I'd ever understood what "double take" actually meant. The guy's eyes almost bugged out, as if I was standing naked on his doorstep.

"Sex hair," he muttered, grabbing my hand and yanking me inside before pressing me up against the wall and kissing me fiercely.

Oh, this was a side effect I *really* liked! I wrapped my arms around him and kissed him back just as hungrily, only to have him groan and slowly but firmly disentangle himself from me, eyes wide and hungry as he stepped away.

"You are dangerous on the best days," he informed me, holding his hands up in a 'surrender' pose. "Wear your hair like that in class, though, and we're going to put on a show for everybody." Shaking his head, he nodded at the kitchen. "Come on, gorgeous. I made us appetizers."

Still high on that soft, fluffy love cloud, I sailed into the kitchen behind him, admiring how good he looked in plain old jeans and an old worn T-shirt. Before I could contemplate the skin beneath them too much, Austin handed me a champagne flute, already filled to the brim with sparkling amber liquid.

He picked up his own flute and tapped mine. "Here's to you, Hannah. In case you aren't aware of it, you're amazing." And he drank as I stood there and bubbled and fizzed every bit as much as the champagne before finally taking a sip.

"So, what's for dinner?" I asked him, looking around at the array of unfamiliar things on the counter.

"Buttermilk curry," he replied, walking over to the counter and handing me a mortar and pestle. "You grind these …" he handed me various spices, "and I'll start to sweat the curry leaves."

"How is this getting to know me, exactly?" I inquired, examining the unfamiliar kitchen device, followed by the spices. I had an overall idea of how it worked, obviously. I'd just never used one of the smashy things before.

"Easy. While you grind and I sweat, we talk."

"There are other places we could do those things," I teased, turning into Annie suddenly.

Austin chuckled. "Yeah, I'm into you, Hannah. Oh yeah." He turned the stove on and reached for what was apparently a curry leaf. "So. Graduation's around the corner. Had any meltdowns yet?"

Tentatively pouring a few grains of—uh, black mustard seed?—into the mortar thing and then wondering if there even were any (they were so small, so I added a bunch more until they were actually visible to the naked eye), I replied, "You could call them that. It's so weird to think the whole world is going to change in a matter of months. No more safe daily schedule, knowing exactly when and where to be at any given time. The worst part is, I actually really like it here on this campus. I'd love to do something here. But I know without a PhD, that's not happening."

He nodded. "Yeah, colleges are hard places to get jobs without higher-level degrees. But you never know. Something could turn up. Hey, are you going to grind those seeds or not?"

"Kinda ... not sure ... how ..."

Laughing, he dropped a lid over the pan and walked over. Sliding his arms around me from behind, he guided my hand to the pestle and whispered in my ear, "Did you plan this?"

No ...

"Yep." I grinned up at him and stole a kiss before refocusing on how he was working the pestle, smoothly grinding each seed into a fine powder. Since he was doing such a great job, I could've easily just leaned back into him and let him do the work, but I did actually want to contribute something tonight, so I reluctantly took over after a moment.

Maybe it was my imagination, or maybe Austin moved a little closer. "So since you have to leave this place, where to next?"

"Probably straight into a master's program," I admitted. "I've been accepted at a few places and—"

"Already?" he interrupted, spinning me around abruptly. "Damn, you're a rockstar." And he kissed me long and slow, sending me right back to Euphoria Land.

"Mmm ... but ... those places will take me away from here," I murmured eventually, as the pungent scent of chilis began to fill the room.

"We'll make it work," he murmured back, before breaking away with such reluctance that I smirked and moving back to tend the stove. I turned back to the spices.

"Why didn't you apply here?" he asked, reaching for a spatula.

"Not enough scholarship money." I found my rhythm, finally, and worked my way quickly through the various spices.

"Want me to see if I can pull a few strings?"

I smiled. "That's crazy sweet, but I really want to do this on my own. You know?"

"I do know. And I love it."

12

CHAPTER TWELVE

The woman drove me flat out crazy. She drove me crazy when she walked in with those curls tumbling every which way and just the slightest hint of makeup on her beautiful face, plus that crop top, which screamed for me to press my lips to her soft warm skin. She drove me crazy when she was clueless in the kitchen: first with the spices, later with chopping scallions and every other small culinary task that I just did naturally, after years of cooking for me and Danny.

She drove me crazy as she informed me that even though I could definitely probably pull strings—they wouldn't even be unwarranted strings; the woman was seriously worth a decent scholarship, given the quality of work she consistently produced — she wanted to pull her own weight. So crazy hot. And she drove me craziest when we finished cooking, let the curry simmer, so the spices would really flavor it, and settled in the living room.

She took a seat on the couch and I, even though I really should've sat all the way across the room, sat between her legs. While we talked, she started massaging my shoulders, and the weirdest thing was—I could tell she wasn't trying to be sexy. She just noticed that I was kind of wound up, and after finding out about Vanessa and all that crap, she decided to try to help me unwind. Not that her hands anywhere on me could remotely accomplish that, but the point was her thoughtfulness. Also her small, strong hands moving across my shoulders firmly ...

"What were we talking about?" I managed to ask finally.

Her laughter moved across me like a tongue of flame. Oh, don't think about tongues, Austin. Bad idea. So very bad.

"I was telling you about my family and how they think it's funny I'm considering being a professor, after I gave my own teachers so much crap. God, I was such a demon."

"You? Never," I said in surprise, tipping my head back to look into her lovely face.

"Oh yeah," she assured me. "I had an attitude you'd have to have heard to believe. That, plus an overall refusal to do homework for half my academic career. It's a miracle I wasn't expelled."

"What changed?" I inquired, reaching up to pull her down for a soft kiss. Her responsive little moan hit me in all the right places.

"I got this civics teacher, Mr. Thomas," she whispered into my lips, stroking her fingers across my five o'clock shadow. "He saw something in me that others didn't, for some reason. He pulled me aside and read me the riot act one day. Other teachers had done that, but not like he did. He just laid it out, how other people wished they had my brains and how I was throwing it all away. How I was an entitled little brat who knew I could get by with mediocre, so I never reached higher."

"Wow." My fingers wove through her beautiful hair. "And that did the trick?"

"Mmmhmm. Don't know why, but it did. I changed my

stripes after that and got my act together enough the last two years of high school to get some decent college money."

To hell with it. Reaching up, I lifted her body off the couch and onto my lap. Grinning like a Cheshire Cat, Hannah curled up into me like she was made to be exactly there, in my arms, against my chest, her head pillowed on my bicep.

"I bet you've changed a few students' lives like that," she told me seriously, as I tried to remember talking. Talking. Talking. Why had I ever come up with that stupidest of all ideas again?"

"I don't know," I admitted. "Every now and then you get one who comes back and says something, but most often you just do your best and give it your all, hoping something works. Did you ever thank Mr. Thomas?"

She frowned. "No, actually. Wow. That's messed up."

"Nah. Most non-teachers wouldn't think of it," I reassured her.

"No, it's awful. He really picked me up out the gutter I was sinking into. I should track him down and say thanks," she insisted, which just made me love her all the more.

Wait. What?

"You said something about a sports scholarship in your own college days. What happened with that?" she asked, toying with the collar of my shirt.

Did I just think it? The l-word? So soon? Holy shit ...

"Austin?"

My nerves were jangling so loudly I was surprised she didn't hear them. "Uh, yeah. Sports. I played golf. Nothing exciting like being a quarterback or anything. But I was pretty good."

Sniffing, I pretended that there was something off in the kitchen, because there was something off in my brain, and I didn't know how to handle it. "Whoa. I better go check. I think the curry's about done."

She willingly got up and I tried not to stumble too much on

my way to the kitchen, especially not when she followed, tucking her hand comfortably into the back of my jeans, again, not in a sexy way, just in a super comfortable, I belong here way.

Which made it all the sexier.

"And you decided not to pursue it any further?" she asked, as I lifted the lid on the curry and examined the pale golden liquid bathing lamb that I'd already partially cooked in the CrockPot earlier, to speed things along.

"Pursue—uh, yeah. I mean, no. It wasn't really a decision. I was good, but not great. There just wasn't any chance I'd make it professionally. And I really did like academics."

"You made a difference in this student's life," she said softly.

Damn it to hell. There was that lurch in my heart again. I had no idea what to do with it, or with the l-word that was dancing around my brain like a demented flea, hitting erogenous zones simultaneously with the amygdala, triggering a wave of hunger and simultaneous fear.

So I turned off the stove and kissed Hannah long and deep, burying myself in her mouth in an attempt to bury the sudden jitters in my brain. When she wrapped around me with wholehearted willingness, I let everything else go except how much I wanted her and how much she obviously wanted me.

HOURS LATER—MANY hours later—with the dawn creeping through the curtain and Hannah snoring softly beside me, my brain re-engaged and with it came the sudden panic.

Oh my God. I loved her. I loved this woman who was not only my student but also years younger than me, someone Danny would view more as a sister than a mother—why was I even considering having Danny think of her as a mother?? He had one of those. Granted, she was a bitch, but she was still his mom. And yet, Hannah would—

Stop it. Stop it!

Sliding out of Hannah's warm embrace, I made a beeline for the shower and stood under a deliberately freezing cold spray. But even before I stepped into it, I was already shivering.

13
CHAPTER THIRTEEN

eeks later

I'M NOT sure where I thought I would be at the end of my senior year of college, but it sure as hell wasn't here. Facing finals, graduation, and finding a job, I was scared, excited, full of trepidation, eager ...

And I was pissed as hell at Austin Fucking Parks.

It was the last thing I expected. The night we spent together was so sweet, maybe in some ways even sweeter than the first time, because now I knew enough to at least participate more fully. And in between heated, hungry bouts, he'd hold me so tightly, his face pressed to my hair, his heart beating fiercely against my chest so I could feel it. I could feel him inside me even when he wasn't, in my mind. In my heart.

But when I woke up the next day, he wasn't there. I found him in the kitchen, viciously scrubbing pans that didn't need scrubbing. We hadn't used them for our dinner. And when I playfully suggested we have curry for breakfast, since we hadn't even tasted it, preferring to taste each other instead, Austin got a strange, faraway look in his eyes. He still glanced heatedly at me, desire licking me like flames. But there was something clouded over it. Suddenly, he stared at me as if I were a ghost.

Before I could figure out why the change or even ask him, he hurried me out of the apartment, mumbling some excuse about how he had to pick up Danny and I probably had somewhere to be, anyway. In my bliss, I barely even clocked his behavior. Yeah, something was off, but I didn't dwell on it. I was too happy.

I only started to get concerned when, from that day on, Austin started canceling the times I was supposed to take Danny for the day. He cut my hours in half, each time with some cool excuse or reason that I shouldn't come that day. I talked myself down from asking him about it. Besides, it really wasn't any of my business and I didn't know anything at all about what it meant to be a parent. I convinced myself that there was nothing at all to be worried about. Although, I did notice that the times that I was taking care of Danny, Austin was as far away from us as he could possibly be, and always dismissed me shortly after arriving. And then Austin told me that he'd "let me know" when or if he needed me to watch Danny again. Of course, he never did.

I didn't want to seem needy, but the truth was I felt wounded by his behavior, with absolutely no explanation or attempt to tell me what had changed for him. I wondered if he regretted everything. But ... why? Had I done something wrong to alarm him? Had I maybe seemed to young in our conversation? Or maybe getting to know me ... he hadn't really liked me. I desperately didn't want to believe that.

So I texted him a few times, trying cautiously to elicit some sort of response. I started with casual hellos and heys. But then I finally asked him if he was avoiding me. I added a little "lol" at the end to add some irony and self-effacing humor. But still, nothing. In class, he seemed to jump in at the last final moment to avoid having time where I could corner him and talk to him, and leaving as soon as the clock struck his time.

As he stood at the blackboard, reading poetry, or taking notes, or writing something with his back to us, the red marker poking out of his back pocket, I tried several times to make eye contact with him. As usual, and like magnets, his eyes always seemed automatically drawn to mine in any crowd. But now, they flitted away fast as the wind, and he would instantly busy himself with something else.

I tried a few more times, lingering after class, hoping he'd wait like before till people were gone and then approach me, but he always hurried away with some kind of muttered excuse.

It took a while for my broken heart to figure things out, but finally the message was received. He didn't want me anymore. I focused very hard on not allowing the revelation to devastate me. And I did a pretty good job. As I said, we had no accord about what the relationship should be or how we should treat each other or what we were to each other. And I'd jumped head-first into this entanglement with him, dashing all of the consequences or conflicts of interest we both had.

Okay, no, that's a lie. I didn't do a good job. He smashed my heart to smithereens and I cried about it more times than I could count, always in the shower so Annie wouldn't notice. She was suspicious anyway, but I managed to head her off because we had bigger fish to fry. With the semester coming to a close, we both had a lot to think about.

I put Austin out of my mind as much as I could. I needed to put myself first, not think about what he was doing. Although ... I couldn't deny that I was concerned. It'd be one thing if he just wanted to kick me to the curb as soon as he was done with me. But it was a whole other thing that he seemed to be trying to fall off the face of the earth in the process. This mystery could easily have been solved by him communicating with me a little bit ... but whatever. His loss.

And mine, the sad little voice kept whispering in the shower and into my pillow every day.

So, imagine my surprise when two weeks out from graduation, Dean Arthur intercepted me after one of my advanced communications courses. I smiled kindly at him, assuming he wasn't there to see me in any way. But the smile slipped when I saw him walking directly towards me.

"Hannah Cosgrove?" he asked.

I felt my heart jump in my chest. It was unavoidable: my thoughts instantly went to Austin. Were we found out? Had he admitted it to someone? I shook my head, dismissing the thought. It didn't help me to assume, so I schooled my features, trying to look as neutral as possible.

"Yes. How can I help you, Dean Arthur?"

"Please, call me Harry. Do you have a moment to talk before your next engagement?"

"Yeah." I could feel my brow furrowing. Why did he talk like a Regency-era love interest?

Dean Arthur pulled me aside into a small alcove in the hallway of the academic building. So, he had no desire to publicly denounce me or accuse me or humiliate me. This, at least, I thought was a good sign.

I couldn't help but blurt out some of my anxiety. "Is this because of my academic performance or requirements? Because I assure you, there should be absolutely no problems there—"

He silenced me by raising his hand. "I actually am here because of your academic performance. But there's hardly a problem. Actually, quite the opposite."

I silently exhaled a breath I hadn't realized I was holding. Some of the anxiety lifted from my shoulders, but I was still wary of the situation. Dean Arthur seemed to be pausing for effect, searching my face for a reaction with impish glee. He reminded me in that moment of a particularly good actor performing as Santa Claus.

"Sir?" I prompted.

"How would you like to take on a fellowship with the university and work as a TA here?" he asked.

I could feel my jaw drop. "What?"

"Your academic record is impeccable, and you clearly show an affinity for and excellence here in the liberal arts college. I'm currently filling some open TA positions for next academic year and I have it on good authority that you're a hard worker. So, what do you say?"

I breathed for a moment. It was an enormous offer. I opened my mouth to sputter a response, but was instantly silenced by him talking over me.

"Now, I know what you're going to say. You're a journalist. What role could you play in academia? Well, I could really use the help, and it's only part time. But it might be something good and stable while you work on starting your writing career."

It did sound amazing. Almost too amazing. "It is an incredible offer. May I ask, which role am I being considered for, specifically?"

"Well, it really all depends on your application. I was considering Professor Soto for his film communications class. But you've never taken that one, and I think you may actually be a better fit to TA for Dr. Parks and his Victorian literature class."

I was sure my poor heart couldn't take anymore beat skipping, yet here I was. Just hearing Austin's name caused me to lose my breath.

"Austin Parks?"

"Yes."

"What did he say?" I pressed, perhaps a bit too earnestly.

"Now, I can't tell you about the confidence between two men of academia, but I can assure you that he only had good things to say about you. And he's not one to sing someone's praises who doesn't deserve it."

I stared at the tops of my shoes. "You're right. He's not."

"Well?"

I looked up, pasting a smile onto my face. "This is exciting news. Could I ask for some time to think about it? I want to make sure it's the best fit and the best choice for me."

"Absolutely," he purred. "But don't leave me waiting long. I'm trying to pin down these hires before graduation."

"Of course. Thank you, sir."

We shook hands and I watched him strut away, quite satisfied with himself that he'd surprised me. *Surprised* was the wrong word. I was shocked. I needed answers. And I knew the only person in this damn city who could give me any.

I DIDN'T EVEN BOTHER KNOCKING on his office door. It was called "open office hours," anyway. It did occur to me that he might be meeting with another student, but I tried to find my inner boss, telling myself that if he refused to meet with me, I would make him talk to me.

He seemed unsurprised when I opened the door. He was sitting at his desk, reading papers with his glasses propped up on the end of his nose. Those damn glasses. I couldn't help but feel my heart leap into the back of my throat. I convinced myself it was from nervousness, not from how strangely cute I found them.

He looked up at me casually. His eyes widened before he was able to school his features into the neutral look he always carefully had when he looked at me. I felt a little self-satisfied that I had affected him at all. I gripped the final in my hands, slightly wrinkling the paper.

"Finals?" I asked him, proud of how even I was able to keep my voice.

He gestured to a wire document tray at the edge of his desk and deliberately looked down at his papers, flipping the same one over multiple times. I walked on leaden feet to the end of his desk, slowly placing my paper down on the pile of others. For a breathless moment, I stood there, staring at the side of his face, which was very specifically looking everywhere except at me. I bit my lip, a little insulted that even when he and I were alone, he couldn't at least talk to me. But what did I expect?

I was ready to give up. I turned toward the door, my legs taking a crazily long time to cooperate with me. About a foot away from the door, my anger and confusion flared up again. This was probably the last time I was ever going to see or speak to him. I deserved answers. In fact, my future and career probably depended on it. I spun around on my heels. I could feel my face fall open, not even bothering to pretend I was unaffected by him.

"Did you tell the Dean to offer me that job?" I blurted out.

He looked up at me, allowing the shock to show plainly on his face this time. "I—"

"He came up to me yesterday and offered me a job, to be your TA. And I was wondering just what the hell you think you're doing."

He looked down again. "I didn't know that he was hiring someone to work for me specifically."

"Bullshit."

He glared at me, his jaw tightening. "He asked me what I thought about you as a student. What would you want me to say? Would you want me to lie?"

"As a student. Right. Did you fuck me as a student as well?"

"Jesus Christ, Hannah! Keep your voice down."

I hated him cursing at me as much as I hated the tone of his voice, so totally devoid of emotion and frozen. "I will not!"

"What do you want me to say?"

"Just tell me the truth, Austin! Did you just use me? Is that what that night was?"

Slowly, he got up from his desk. He took one, two, three steps toward me, and reached forward. I closed my eyes, already ready for his touch, his kiss, anything to end this cold war between us.

Instead, he gripped the doorknob behind me and opened his office door.

"Get out," he ordered in a cold voice. When I opened my eyes, still too afraid and stunned to move, he repeated himself. "I said get out."

The remains of my heart crumbled.

So this was how it was going to be. And I realized I didn't want to fight him. I just wanted answers. And he wouldn't even give me those.

"Goodbye," I whispered, and left his office, not looking back for a second. My feet carried me down the hallway, out of the building, across the quad, and into the university auditorium. At the end of the semester, it felt almost completely abandoned. Only a few working lights were left on and there wasn't a soul around.

It was here, among the empty seats in the hushed quiet of a large, silent place, that I allowed myself one last cry over Austin Fucking Parks. After this, I promised myself, there would be no more. I was done.

The worst part was that I wasn't even angry anymore. I was just so very numb.

"He did what??!"

I finally gave up and told Annie. It was just too hard to keep hiding everything.

"Son of a bitch!" she yelled, stomping over to my side of the room and pulling me into a hug, which would have started me crying except that I was now completely empty of tears. "Oh, honey," she said sympathetically, pulling back. "I'll poison him for you. Something slow and painful."

I managed a half laugh. "Thanks, I think. But if you get put away for murder, then I'm really all alone forever."

"Don't say that," she admonished. "You're not alone now and you never will be. You'll always have me. And there'll be a much better guy out there for you. One who knows everything you're worth and treats you like a queen."

I wished I could believe her. Truthfully, I had no interest in being royalty. All I wanted was the guy who was definitely no prince.

14

CHAPTER FOURTEEN

I didn't think it was possible for me to drink as much as I had, and yet, here we are. Leo watched me knock back whiskey after whiskey on the rocks, drunk so fast that the room-temperature booze barely had time to cool down on the ice. I couldn't understand why I didn't feel the least bit drunk, and I complained as much to him.

He shrugged. "I don't know ... are you depressed?" he asked, knowing full well the answer.

It didn't take a psychologist to realize I was headed off the deep end. Between the deep circles under my eyes and the grimace on my lips that came from more than just the booze, I was about the worst person in the world to hang out with. In fact, I might just be the worst person in the world, period.

The things I'd realized I felt for Hannah that night had been things I'd never felt for anyone, including Vanessa. I loved Danny with my whole heart, but other than him, I didn't know what it meant to be completely overwhelmed by another person, to the point that not having them in my life left me bereft. I finally realized that Vanessa hadn't been entirely to blame in our marriage; she'd undoubtedly felt my lack of real love, as much as I'd felt the lack of hers.

I loved Hannah. There was no denying it. And after the bed sheets had cooled and her breathing became heavy with sleep, I had still lain awake, staring at the ceiling. I'd realized in that moment that somewhere between the game of chicken that she and I had been playing for months and the affirmation of our attraction to one another, my feelings for her had bloomed from plain desire into something more.

This revelation would seem joyous to some, exciting to others. To me, it was terrifying. I had never been a person to catch feelings. And yes, I'd had trysts with many women, but it was never more than a heated encounter or a night of fun. I'd never had a problem with separating those two halves of myself. Perhaps the fact that Hannah had borne witness to my duality of self was partially to blame for the development. She had seen me in my raw, desirous state. But she had also seen me in my relationship with my son.

And of course, she had to be my fucking student. I pushed down the larger feelings to find only shame and self-loathing underneath. What was I thinking? I couldn't believe how stupid I'd been. Sleeping with a student, involving her in my son's life. What was I going to do when this all blew up in my face?

That was the issue. I chose to believe that if she had been any other woman who I was dating, without the ramifications of possible career repercussions for me and academic repercussions for her, it would have been okay to love her. I almost convinced myself of that, except I wasn't that good of a liar. It was more than her student status that was freaking me out. I just had no idea at all how to love anybody. Shit. Shit. Shit.

I was unable to catch more than a few hours of sleep that night, my disturbing thoughts keeping me up until I could see the first tendrils of growing sunlight outside of my window. I resisted the ache to wake Hannah up so I could ask her how she felt, too. Were her emotions changing, too? Was it just me? I didn't want to project any of my confusion onto her. This was her first time doing this. Hell, it felt like my first time doing this.

I couldn't just be a teacher to her anymore, no matter what the outcome. I now realized that we'd been trying for months to compartmentalize these different parts of our relationship when they were really all one and the same.

I had two options in front of me. The first was to sort through my feelings and then present them to Hannah with an open mind, knowing that I could be rejected by her but hoping beyond hope that she and I were somehow on the same page. The second was to ignore everything I was feeling and bail, something that I was suspecting I should've done that very first day when I realized the girl from the club was also one of my students.

I was leaning heavily toward the first option when I hurried Hannah out of my apartment the next morning. My traitorous body begged me not to, wanting to ask her to stay, to talk, to snuggle, to go another round or three. But I needed space. I needed air.

But the second option began to look amazing when, just as I was about to leave to pick Danny up from his sleepover, Vanessa arrived in my apartment.

"Don't think I didn't see that," she coyly insinuated. Between her tone, her facial expression, and the fact that she freely entered my space *again* unannounced and uninvited, I was instantly on edge.

"What are you doing here?" I demanded, refusing to play whatever game she was starting with me.

"I saw that twenty-something leaving your place this morning."

My eyes narrowed. "Are you following me? Or watching me? Because that is beyond creepy."

She laughed at me, a completely cold laugh. A vision of Hannah floated before my eyes: her genuine smiles glittering in the darkness of my apartment by moonlight, or giving me a thrill to see her among the other faces in class. I blinked, returning to the dead, leery eyes in front of me.

"Austin, please," she said, rolling her eyes, as if I was in on some joke between the two of us. "You can stop with this. I know what you're doing."

With that, she took two long steps, gripped the sides of my face, and pressed her lips against mine. As soon as she began, I ended it with a firm press of my arms against her shoulders. I felt the rage rise in the back of my throat.

"What are you doing?"

"Oh, come on. I tell you I'm moving back to town and then you parade your student around in front of me. I get it, you can have whoever you want."

"Jesus, Vanessa. It's none of your business and it has nothing to do with you."

"It's exactly how you courted me the first time."

I couldn't even believe this. "What are you talking about?" I said, throwing my arms up in the air.

"Remember our sophomore year, when you came to my sorority mixer and you started making out with Maria Smith because you wanted me to know that you were available and sexy?"

"First of all, I made out with Maria because she liked me too and I wanted to get laid that night. Second of all, why the fuck would you think for a second that anything I do with someone else has anything to do with you?"

"Remember how good we were together?" she said. "We made Danny. We owe it to him to at least give it a shot."

"We gave it a shot years ago," I retorted. "Until you decided that you didn't want to do any of the heavy lifting that being a parent really entails." I rubbed my eyes with the heels of my hands. "You know what? I'm done here."

"Are you seriously telling me that you'd rather sleep with that nothing girl instead of be with me, the mother of your child?" Ah, there was the Vanessa I knew. The pettiness, the childishness, the raw and awful anger.

"I'm telling you that my life is absolutely none of your business, and what I am or am not doing with Hannah is none of your business. And we aren't together." I yanked my coat on. "Now, if you'll excuse me, I need to pick up our son from his sleepover, so I'm going to have to ask you to get the fuck out of my house."

I ushered her out my door, made sure to lock it behind us, and barreled down the street, ignoring Vanessa's cry behind me. Danny's friend's house was only two stops on the L away, but I decided to walk the distance anyway. I needed to clear my head. Vanessa was crazy. I had always known that. But I had a moment when I realized what Hannah and I looked like to someone on the outside looking in. Her, a younger student, and me, her divorced single dad professor, making moves on her. Vanessa misread everything about me, but I realized how easy it would be to misread the whole situation.

And did I want this? Did I want to put my little family, including my son, and my career on the line to be with someone I'd had a few nights of passion with? I could sense that was what was happening between Hannah and me, but in that moment, I was terrified by the whole prospect. She was young and beautiful. It wouldn't be hard for her to find someone else to replace me. That was what was best for both of us. And me? What would I find? I tried not to think about how no one could ever replace her.

I didn't trust myself to talk to her, so I allowed myself to slowly float away. I knew that what I was doing was referred to as "ghosting" and was, even in younger groups, kind of a shitty thing to do, but I needed Hannah to move on. I needed her to leave at the end of the semester and never look back. She had to see that it would be better that way. I was a coward. No denying it. Who does that to anyone, much less a total innocent?

So it broke me when she confronted me in my office, looking as glorious as I had ever seen her, not holding back her frustration and anger. Why? She wanted to know why I was doing this. Again, I was completely torn. Part of me reached out to her and wanted to soothe her and explain what was happening. The other part of me held me back, reminding me that I shouldn't talk to her. I was bad for her. I was dangerous. This was too much and neither of us should have to pretend that we could do this for one more day.

Which was why I was downing yet another drink, with Leo watching judgmentally.

"You are a royal mess."

"It's the only way I'm ever going to be royalty, so why not." The booze burned as it hit the back of my throat and I knew I was going to pay dearly tomorrow, but it didn't matter. At the very least for a few hours I might be able to stop feeling.

"Okay, Prince Not-So-Charming. So, do you want to talk about it yet?"

"Go fuck yourself," I hissed in response.

"Fine, drink alone. See if I care." Usually, I could take Leo's ribbing, but I could tell that this remark was different from his normal jabs. He seemed to really mean it. I believed that he would get up and leave me here to drink alone, just like he said. Maybe it was because he could sense the depth and meaning behind my harshness. Maybe he'd just had quite enough of my shit.

"I'm sorry. I don't know what to do. You're not the one I'm angry at," I apologized.

He snorted and smiled at me. "Don't worry, big guy; you're not going to get rid of me so easily. Especially when things are just about to get more exciting."

I looked up at him in confusion and he nodded at something over my shoulder, a flirty smile plastered to his lips. I turned and could feel my eyes widen. "Oh, shit."

Out of the crowd of the bar, Hannah's friend was barreling toward me. Annie. The rage on her face was unmistakable, and besides, I didn't tend to forget the names of people who insulted me on every single level. *Oh, shit* was right. I didn't have it in me to deal with this today. I popped an ice cube in my mouth and broke it apart with my teeth, giving my anxiety and hatred something to do when the redhead came to stop in front of me, arms crossed. Ever the charmer, Leo was more than happy to fill the tense silence.

She arrived at my table shooting daggers at me with her eyes. Not just daggers. Hand grenades. Machine gun fusillades. She shot me, knifed me, poisoned me, all with one furious glare.

"Annie! Looking beautiful as always."

"You son of a bitch." She picked up my almost empty glass and poured the few dregs over my head. "You lousy, good for nothing piece of shit!

"Go fuck yourself," I snarled, grabbing for a napkin and swiping at my damp hair.

"Bartender!" she yelled. "Another of whatever he was drinking."

Leo's face was just a bit too excited. "By all means. Keep giving it to him, Annie. He deserves it. The bastard."

Annie shot him the dirtiest look possible and then aimed her ire back on me, her nostrils flaring. "Do you remember what I told you a month ago?"

"That I didn't deserve your friend? Yeah, you were right about that."

"Not that, you shit. I told you that if you do anything to hurt her, I would come after you." Her eyes flashed. "She really liked you, you know that?"

I forced my words to come out as ice, however much she had every right to be furious at me. "We wanted each other; we had each other. That's the end of it. Could you buzz off? I'd like to drown my sorrow over here in peace."

"Oh, that's real rich. Like you deserve a single wink of sleep tonight." The drink arrived and I backed away but way too late as she hurled it right in my face.

I spluttered and scrubbed at my burning eyes.

Great friend that he was, Leo jumped in, overtly aroused by her aggressiveness. "If you'd like to stay up and make sure he can't sleep, I can always think of a way that you and I can pass the time ... naked."

Annie made a face. "What the fuck is wrong with you? Were you dropped on your head as a child?"

"Almost certainly," I responded, raising my hand to get the bartender's attention. So I was soaking wet. Screw it. I still wasn't damn near drunk enough to go numb.

It was a bad call to speak up, because Annie turned back to me and went back to the business of tearing me a new one, which was something that, unlike my colleague, I was not in any way turned on by.

"Nobody asked you," she snapped. "But I could ask you the same question. What the hell is wrong with you? I get that you weren't dating officially or anything, but you can't deny you two were dancing around it. So then you don't even call? Not even an email? No explanation whatsoever for why almost the moment you take a girl's virginity, you completely fall off the face of the planet? And what you did to her in your office ..."

"I didn't hear about that. What'd he do?" Leo inquired.

"Treated her like a whore," she said bluntly, which actually did make me wince. Had I really been that bad? Reading my thoughts, she snapped, "Yeah, that's exactly what you did. You might as well have thrown money at her!"

I flushed. "Now wait a minute—"

"No, you wait," she cut me off. "You good for nothing scumbag. I don't even have enough adjectives or cuss words to describe how low you are. You broke my best friend's heart in the worst possible way. You won't even have the decency to talk to her and explain *why*, so now you're fucking well going to tell me. What's your deal? What's your beef? Why are you being such a massive asshole?"

"Because I think I'm falling in love with her, okay?" I shouted, causing a hush to fall over the bar. There seemed to be no air amongst the three of us, robbed by the impact of my statement.

"Whoa, seriously?" Annie blustered, clearly not expecting this development. I ignored her, accepting another drink from the bartender ... what number was it again? It didn't matter. I drank it down anyway. Maybe I actually was feeling the booze. I didn't generally go around yelling that I loved people. Or even admitting it to myself, apparently.

Leo had a rare showing of his ability to charm an awkward situation, as opposed to making it worse. "Annie," he said calmly. "Would you please excuse my friend and I for a second? We need to have a private conversation."

Some of her anger returned, but a strange sort of compassion lay underneath. I wondered if, despite all her bravado, she could sympathize with me. I wondered if she'd ever found herself in a similar situation.

"You're an idiot," she told me harshly. "But if you're in love with her, and you really mean that when you say that you are, then you should tell her. She deserves to know. But I honestly don't believe you love her, or you wouldn't be treating her this way. Otherwise you're just about the world's worst human being."

With that, she turned and left. Leo watched her as she left, and I wondered what I would have to do to convince the bartender I was good for another one, even though I had yelled to the point of silencing his whole bar.

"Do you want to talk about it now?" Leo pressed, a rather fatherly look on his face.

"Not really," I spat out.

"Did you really do what she said in your office?"

"Yes! Damn it. Yes, I did. But I didn't mean it that way." Guilt ate a hole in my gut and the alcohol buzzing through me made that hole ache and sting like a mother. Unfortunately that pain did nothing to ease the other pain from the realization of what I'd done.

Leo laughed totally humorlessly. "Oh, so that makes it okay? You're better than that, Austin. Look, fucking is one thing, but falling in love is a completely different animal," Leo insisted. I rolled my eyes. I hated when he developed a conscience at my literal lowest moment.

"So what do you want me to do? I already fucked up things between us," I argued.

"If she feels the same way, she will forgive you. Even though you're being an ass," Leo responded. "Women are good like that. Because believe me, if a girl treated me that way, I'd never darken her doorstep again. Way too much pride.

"I can't love her! There are too many reasons why it will never work!"

"You really are an ass," he said in obvious surprise. "Not just an ass, but a coward to boot. Here I thought I was the shallow jerk in this relationship. Huh. Goes to show you never really know someone. Bartender, another one, please. When did you get so low, Austin?"

I shrugged morosely. "I don't know. Hanging around you, probably."

"Oh no. Don't pin it on me. Because you see, I own what an ass I am. Whereas you go around pretending to be better than everyone else."

The drink arrived and before I knew what was happening, he'd upended it over my head. "You deserve way worse than that," my best friend observed, and got up and walked away, sticking me not only with the drink running down my hair and face in rivulets, but with the entire tab, even for his own shots. Ah, SHIT!

I WASN'T SPRUNG into action until Danny and I were playing with some of his action figures later that day.

"Is Hannah mad at me?" he asked abruptly.

I stopped in my tracks, disturbed by the question.

"Of course not, buddy. Why would you think that?"

"Well, she stopped hanging out with me. She didn't even say goodbye. So I was worried she was mad at me."

I could feel my heart breaking, not just for me, but for my son. I felt a new tide of disappointment rising, but swallowed it down in an attempt to compose myself for the sake of my child.

"Hannah is graduating soon. She's just busy, buddy. It has nothing to do with you." At least that last part had been honest.

"Well, I miss her." For such a benign thing to say, it completely cut me to my core. And it made me feel that there was something I needed to do. I had known I had to do it for, honestly, about a week, but this was the final straw. There was only one thing left to do.

CHAPTER FIFTEEN

I hated being in my apartment alone. Sure, being a writer, I always liked my solitary time, but after a while, it always became a sinkhole of unproductivity. Perhaps part of it was due to the fact that I wasn't used to having so little to do. Since all my classes had wrapped up, I'd spent the last week planning for graduation, welcoming my family coming to town for the event, and making arrangements and reservations for post-grad celebrations.

Now was the proverbial calm before the storm. My entire life was relegated to re-watching my favorite sitcoms, drinking wine with Annie, and avoiding most other people. I knew that next week would be crazy, so I guess in a way I was preparing myself for the craziness to come by embracing the quietness of my life.

And at this moment, I was preparing for it literally and physically as well. The new heels I would be wearing to accept my diploma were strapped to my feet. Over the phone, my mom had assured me that wearing them to walk would be so much easier if I spent a few days moving around in them and stretching them out. I was mostly just using it as an excuse to avoid cooking and keep my quiet existence. Which was also why I had started my third puzzle today in the crossword book I'd picked up from the bodega this morning. I knew how I looked, splayed across the couch, doing a crossword, with dressy heels strapped onto my feet. I enjoyed how comical it all was, which was something I couldn't take for granted after all the drama with Austin. I was doing my best to move on and stop thinking about him, but my heart was still more than a little sore.

When I heard the knock at my door, I assumed that it couldn't be anything other than the pizza I'd ordered.

"Just a sec!" I called out, struggling to extricate myself from my complicated shoes. I sighed with relief as each foot was released, finally. I hobbled to the door on bruised feet, fumbling with my wallet as I went. I opened the door to see Austin staring back at me. All the air completely left the room. For a moment, I couldn't move, couldn't breathe. I just existed for a moment in some sort of weird limbo. What universe was I in that Austin Parks appeared on my doorstep, days after I'd told him off in his own office?

The first conscious thought that passed through my mind was thinking about what I was wearing. My sweatpants, my hair up in a bun, my stained T-shirt. And I felt as crappy as I looked. To be fair, and to my slight satisfaction, he didn't look any better. He had dark circles under his eyes and looked at me like a kicked dog. His own bad appearance was what ripped the first words out of my mouth to him.

"You look like shit."

His face broke out into a smile and he laughed darkly. God, I'd forgotten how attractive he was. That was a lie. I'd never forgotten it. I just didn't like to think about it.

"So do you," he responded. "Danny misses you, by the way."

Wrong thing to say. *So* the wrong thing to say. I loved the kid, but that was so not what I wanted to hear out of Austin's lips. I started to swing the door shut and he jammed his foot in between before it could close completely.

"Wait. Wait," he said quickly. "Please. Wait."

"Why should I? Give me one good reason."

"I don't have one," he admitted, which surprised me. "Other than ... I miss you, too, Hannah."

Damn it. Okay, that was more in line with what I desperately wanted to hear from him.

"You wouldn't have had to miss me if you hadn't just dumped me like a hot potato," I pointed out. "What are you doing here?"

"You're right. I'm here to apologize."

I narrowed my eyes at him. I could feel my rage rising again inside of me. Who the hell did he think he was, able to come over to my home whenever he wanted? Did he think that everything was just going to be okay? And what the hell could he want from me anyway? But ... the other side of that coin was that perhaps this was finally the explanation that I'd wanted for the past few months. And if I was being honest with myself, I really missed him.

So, still guarded, I stepped to the side and allowed him to come in. Closing the door behind him, I followed him to my couch. He considered sitting for a second before remaining standing. It was strange to see him in my living room. It was the collision between two worlds that both of us had tried to keep separate.

I crossed my arms. I could sense that something big was about to happen, and I wanted to get one more jab in. "So you know, you're an absolute idiot and you've got a lot of nerve to think you could come here."

"I know. You're right." I raised my eyebrow at his instant concession. "But I need to tell you something. And you can't interrupt me, because it's hard for me to say. Can you be okay with that?"

I pursed my lips and nodded. Austin took a deep, steadying breath. With that, he began. "First of all, I am so sorry for what I've done to you the past few weeks, and in my office last week. You deserved an explanation and I know that nothing I can say can excuse what an ass I was. But the reason I did that is because I got scared and I thought it might be best for us to have a clean break and both of us could go on with our lives. And I know that sounds dramatic and weird and we were never really together or anything, so you probably think I'm crazy. But the truth is I realized that I was developing some serious feelings for you. Hannah, I'm afraid to say the word."

I didn't say anything, because I hurt so badly and because what he was saying actually made sense and I wasn't ready to forgive so easily.

"Like, feelings on the level I've never quite felt before, and I was thinking about how you were a student and maybe you just wanted the one night of sexual experience and I felt like I needed to run away, instead of facing the possibility that you didn't feel the same way. And so I'm here now. I'm trying to face it, and I can't believe you're in front of me right now and that you're even listening to me."

"I can't believe I am either," I said quietly. "You hurt me worse than anyone I've ever known, Austin. Losing my virginity was supposed to sting, but you were so good, it almost didn't at all. So you decided to make up for it by making me hurt badly in other ways."

He went white as he obviously thought through my words before answering. "You're right. You're absolutely right. And I can say I'm sorry over and over, but it won't mean anything unless you see it in action."

"What does that mean?" I asked, wrapping my arms around myself and turning my head away a little, because he didn't get to see my tears, damn him.

"It means I'm begging you to forgive me. I'll do anything you ask. Anything at all, if you'll just try to forgive me my total stupidity and give me a second chance." To my total surprise, and maybe to his, who knows, his voice cracked.

A tear slid down my cheek and I got up, clenching my fists. "No. No. Why do you deserve a second chance? Do you have any idea what you've done?" I finally turned to him, letting him see the shadows in my eyes, the tracks of tears on my face, the weight I'd lost from forgetting to eat when I was trying so hard to forget him. "I didn't realize people could be that cruel, Austin. You took my innocence in every sense of the word. My belief in the goodness of people."

"Hannah." He got to his feet and I took a step back involuntarily, afraid he'd reach out. If he touched me, I was done for.

"There is nothing I can say or do," he repeated hoarsely, and this time I didn't miss the shadows in his own eyes. I realized that maybe he'd actually thought about me every now and then. Maybe I wasn't the only one who was suffering.

"I don't deserve another chance, but I'm asking you anyway." Cautiously, Austin took a step toward me, then another, and another. I just barely held my ground and managed to not flee like a scared rabbit as he finally stopped in front of me.

"I'm ... falling in ... love with you," he whispered, and my eyes widened slightly. "I've only ever said that word to my son and his mother, Hannah. And I didn't mean it with Vanessa, even though I thought I did at the time. I'm ... falling for everything about you. Your intelligence. Your kindness. Your sense of humor. Your courage."

"You could say my beauty too," I mumbled, finally breaking and taking my own step toward him.

He opened his arms and finally, finally, finally I was in them, pressed against his chest as he wrapped me up tight and seemed to cling to me as I clung to him. "Of course, your beauty," he whispered into my hair, and the scent of his cologne wrapped around me so familiar and soft that I cried into his chest, letting my tears soak the fabric.

"I'm sorry, baby. I'm so sorry," he said again and again, until my grief finally abated, along with my anger.

I lifted my eyes and looked up into his.

"You really hurt me, Austin," I said quietly. "Don't do it again."

"I won't," he promised.

"I'm still your student."

"It doesn't matter anymore. You and I both know our relationship hasn't affected your grade in the slightest. You've earned your A. I haven't given you a thing." He rested his forehead against mine. "Baby, it doesn't matter. Nothing does, except making it up to you. And I will. I promise."

Strangely enough, I really did believe him. And when he kissed me, it was so tender that I teared up for entirely different reasons than I'd cried all these last weeks. It was because it felt like I was finally home once again. The pieces of the world slid back into place, finally.

CHAPTER SIXTEEN

6 months later

HALFWAY THROUGH A TIRADE about poem structure, I happened to catch sight of my watch and noticed that I had, in fact, made the class go over fifteen minutes. I could feel myself blushing as I apologized to my class profusely and dismissed them. When I got really into a lesson, I could go on and on forever, much to the chagrin of my students. I was really getting in my flow with all of this. Hannah regularly reassured me that everyone found my untimely nature cute.

"But you only say that because you think I'm charming," I argued.

She gave me a toothy grin. "Maybe."

It took time for me to earn back her trust. We didn't even have sex for several months after that first tentative step when she forgave me. It was too important to build other parts of our relationship. So we did things in public places. Restaurants.

Bowling. Movies. Even a stupid pottery painting thing that I sucked at so bad, Hannah laughed the whole night through. I loved it because she finally seemed like Hannah again. I'd mess up a dozen damn mugs if it made her laugh freely.

I didn't even let her keep babysitting Danny, because I wanted her to realize that she was more than a student and a babysitter to me. She was Hannah. My Hannah. The woman that I was more and more comfortable telling myself I loved.

After she graduated and accepted the TA position, she also pulled her own strings with her academic credentials and cobbled together enough money to start working toward a masters right there on campus. It was important to her because she liked being a TA—my TA—but she wanted more too, eventually. And I loved that she did.

At the end of our first semester working together, we decided we'd navigated the situation well enough that we could move in together. Ever the one to know exactly what she wanted, she was ready to go at the end of the summer. She was fully incorporated into my life and Danny's, and she basically was living with me at that point, since she stayed at my place nearly every night.

Hannah still got angry when I got intimidated by what we were building together. And yeah, I still freaked out occasionally. She'd lose her patience, understandably so, and we would fight. And then we would talk through it. My relationship with Hannah was definitely a learning experience, but she was worth it. She was worth all of it.

The best thing I did for our relationship was outing us to Dean Arthur. Right after her graduation, I basically blurted out to him that I was in love with Hannah, a former student and future co-worker, and that nothing he could say would stop me. But Dean Arthur surprised me when he shrugged his shoulders, looking completely unsurprised, and said, "Of course I wouldn't even try."

He then proceeded to tell me that he and his wife had met when he was a lecturer for her master's program. The reason for the rule is to discourage conflicts of interest, but ultimately it wasn't up to the administration to dictate relationships of consenting adults. He asked me if I thought that Hannah had actually not earned her A in my class. I vehemently told him no, and he smoothly said that he didn't see a problem. Just so long as she didn't interfere with my work. I assured him she wouldn't and had kept true to my word ... most of the time.

Later, I enthusiastically relayed the tale to Hannah, still reeling from the story and from Arthur's overwhelming understanding. That was the first time she told me she loved me. And I didn't quite manage to say it back, but she didn't get angry, thank God.

On days Hannah wasn't in class with me, I missed her badly. I'd come to expect her quiet assurance at the front of the room, operating the projector, helping me write things out on the blackboard, and tapping her watch to let me know to wrap it up.

Today I wondered if I should pick up some dinner for us on the way home. I knew she was nose deep in her studies and would appreciate the gesture and not having to cook for a night.

"Baby?" I walked in the door and spotted her immediately, sitting at her desk hunched over her laptop.

She turned and eyed the bags I was carrying. "Pad Thai?" she asked hopefully, sniffing the air.

"Your middle name should be bloodhound," I teased, opening a container and walking over to wave it under her nose.

She groaned happily. "Mmm. I love how you take care of me on days when I'm going crazy with tests and wondering whether I can possibly survive more years of writing essays."

And that was when it happened. Totally naturally. Without any fear at all. I put the Pad Thai down on the floor and leaned in to kiss her.

"You'll survive. And by the way. I love you."

Her eyes filled with tears so fast that I immediately realized how badly she'd been wanting to hear the words, and felt like a first-class heel. But before I could apologize, she was hugging me tight.

"You are so slow at some things," she whispered into my chest. "But waiting as worth it. Tell me again?"

"I love you." It was so easy to say it now that I wondered why it had ever been difficult before. "I love you. I love you. Do you realize that it's almost been a year since you and I first made love?"

Hannah kissed me. "I love you. And yes, I remember. Girls are all about that kind of stuff."

"You seriously remember the date of that?" I asked.

"I distinctly remember subconsciously doodling hearts all over the day in my calendar," she smirked.

"Which do you consider our true anniversary? So I can plan for the future." I felt myself startle at my own words. We'd been together for nearly a year, so it wasn't as if the future had never come up, but it felt more concrete to me in that moment than any other time.

"When you showed up at my place to apologize. That was the real beginning of everything."

"Noted." I wrapped my arm around her waist. "Come let me feed you and then you can get back to cracking the books."

She didn't make it back to the laptop that night, though. We ate and then made love. And when she fell asleep that night, I whispered, "I love you" to her, and it no longer frightened me.

CHAPTER SEVENTEEN

Six more months

So, yeah, I forgave him. And he more than kept his promise, even if sometimes he did have panic attacks so bad that I wondered if he had a side of Hugh Grant-commitment phobia in him. But I never doubted that he'd stay faithful to me. And eventually, I stopped doubting that he'd eventually feel comfortable enough to use the l-word. It took forever, but when it happened, it was perfect.

Damn, I loved the man, from his head to his feet and everything in between, including how great a father he was. I also loved that he wanted me to be a part of Danny's life that was more than just a babysitter. After screwing up so bad, Austin really got it right.

Which was why on this, the anniversary of the day he showed up at my place to apologize, I was almost skipping down the block to our house like a little girl. I knew he'd remember. And he'd have something nice for dinner ... maybe flowers ... I'd had a horrendous test earlier in the day, and there was nothing I could think of that would be better than curling up with my man.

Only, as I walked up to our house, I realized his car wasn't in the driveway. Confused, I tried the door and it was locked, even though when he was home he always made sure to leave it open for me.

I used my own key and stepped inside, finding the house dark and cold, like nobody had been inside all day, not even Danny, who should've been here. It was Austin's weekend for custody.

"Hello?" I called uncertainly, wandering through the kitchen and living room, hoping he was planning a surprise and was going to jump out of nowhere and scare the crap out of me. But there was nothing and nobody. Not so much as a note pinned on the fridge to let me know the deal.

"Well, crap," I said out loud, trying not to feel too hurt. "He forgot." I took a slow breath. Guys just sucked at that stuff, right? No big deal. Deciding I should go right back out instead of staying around moping, I texted Annie, who was working at an attorney's office only a few miles away.

Drinks? On me...

She responded less than two seconds later. *Free booze? Yaaassss! The usual place? I'll be there in 15.*

I looked down at myself and figured I should at least look slightly nicer to go out. Khakis and a boring shirt were my go-tos on exam days, because they required no thought. Hurrying upstairs, I impulsively slipped into a cute LBD, did something random that sort of looked okay with my hair, and even slicked a little lipgloss on while I waited for my Uber.

"Look at you!" Annie exclaimed as I walked into our favorite bar. "All dressed up just for me? Hate to tell you, girl, but I'm taken."

I stopped dead in my tracks at the table she'd held for us. "You what?"

She grinned from ear to ear. "Jeremy finally decided we're dating."

"Hallelujah!" I exclaimed, hugging her hard. We'd been waiting for months for her coworker to see the light. They'd been going out *forever*, but kind of like Austin didn't like l-words, neither did Jeremy. The l-word for him was 'label.' Annie had been surprisingly patient waiting for him to come around.

"Look at you. All labeled officially." I grinned and flagged a bartender down, giving him our usual orders before sitting down across from Annie at the hightop.

"Took him long enough," she grumbled, but I could see how happy she was and it made me happy for her. She'd stuck with me through all of the Austin drama and more than deserved a fair shake at romance now that she'd decided one-night stands weren't what she wanted anymore.

"Where's loverboy?" Annie asked, reaching eagerly for a margarita as the bartender placed it in front of her.

"No idea," I admitted, taking a long sip of my own drink. "This is his weekend with Danny, but neither of them were home. Maybe he had something planned that I forgot about."

"But isn't today ..."

I shook my head. "How do you keep all this stuff in your head?? Yes, it's our sort-of anniversary."

"The guy forgot, huh." She grimaced. "Make him pay."

I laughed. "Why? It's not a huge deal. It would've been nice, yeah, but who really cares?"

"You do ..."

I rolled my eyes. "Yeah, okay. I do. But we're not married or anything, so I guess it doesn't really matter."

"So why don't we get married, and then it'll matter more?"

Austin's voice came out of nowhere, so much so that I nearly jumped out of my seat. Across from me, Annie grinned from ear to ear as I slowly, very very slowly, turned and found my boyfriend down on one knee at the foot of the table. Danny stood beside him, beaming as brightly as Annie.

CHAPTER EIGHTEEN

You were about to get pissed at me for seeming to forget, weren't you ... Let me take a step back here and explain. See, like me, Danny had completely fallen head over heels for Hannah. She was sweet, charming, and had become a stable figure in his life. He'd taken to calling her Momma Hannah, something that moved Hannah so deeply that she had to hide her tears against my chest in fear that Danny would assume he'd said something wrong when, in fact, he'd said something so right.

A few weeks back, Hannah had been studying upstairs for a test while Danny and I made dinner. I was spooning some veggies onto his plate when he blurted, "Dad, when are you gonna marry Hannah?"

I felt myself seize up at the question. This was something we definitely hadn't discussed. "I don't know," I fumbled. "Maybe, maybe not." Honestly, I'd been thinking about it more than a little bit. I just had no idea that Danny was on the same wavelength.

This overly simplified answer didn't satisfy him at all. "Well, I think you should. She needs to stay with us forever, Dad."

After a moment, I slipped away to the house safe and came back with a little black box. "Shhh," I warned Danny, who looked at it curiously, even after I opened it for him to see the sparkler I'd picked out a month ago, when I'd realized no one else would ever be more 'it' for me. Hannah was my heart.

I guess kids don't necessary 'get' wedding rings like adults, because he didn't freak out. Eventually, I explained, "It's what I'm going to give her when I ask her, Dan."

"When you ask her ... ohhhh." His little face broke into a smile like a sunbeam. "Way to go, Dad! And it's kind of glittery. Girls like that."

I hid a grin and pocketed the ring safely. "I hear they do."

So that was two weeks before the anniversary of my apology, and I couldn't figure out what the best time to ask would be, besides that exact day. So Annie and I plotted and schemed ...

And now here I was, down on one knee, with Danny prepared to deliver his lines beside me. He'd insisted on wearing a bowtie and now tugged on it nervously before clearing his throat proudly, drawing a chorus of 'awwws' from bar patrons who were watching curiously.

"Hannah, my dad loves you a whole lot. Like, a whole whole whole lot. I love you too. I want you to be with us forever."

Her eyes filled with tears and I took my turn, reaching for her hand. "He's right. I love you a whole lot. Like, a whole whole whole lot, Hannah. I think I loved you from that first day." We shared a look, remembering that first heated night on the dance floor, when neither of us had a clue we'd end up here one day. "You're the best thing to ever happen to me outside of Danny. I almost threw it away once and I'm never making that mistake again. I love you, Hannah," I said again, gazing up into her eyes and holding out the ring. "Give me a chance and I'll spend my life giving you everything and more."

"You already give me everything," she sniffled, only to have Annie snap, just as tearfully,

"Don't interrupt him, dumbass!"

"She said a bad word, Dad."

"I heard, son."

"Sorry," Annie muttered. "My bad."

Okay, not quite how I'd seen my proposal going ... but a smile lurked at the corner of Hannah's lips, which made me love her all the more.

"Marry me, Hannah. I'll love you forever. Please?"

"Yes!" She threw herself off the barstool and into my arms, almost knocking me over. "Yes, yes, yes, yes!"

As I held her tightly before drawing her into a long, sweet kiss, I heard Danny comment to Annie, "I knew she'd like the glittery thing."

Hannah laughed in my arms and leaned back to pull my son into a one-armed hug, never letting go of me in the process. "I love you, Danny."

Ever the boy, my kid hugged her back fiercely for a second, then reverted to type and squirmed away. "Ewww, Annie. They're kissing. Take me outside?"

And she did, which allowed me to kiss Hannah all the more.

THE END.

SIGN UP TO RECEIVE FREE BOOKS

Sign Up to Receive Free E-Books and Audiobook Codes.

Would you like to read **The Unexpected Nanny, Dirty Little Virgin** and **other romance books** for **free?**

You can sign up to receive these free e-books and audiobooks by typing this link into your browser:

https://www.steamyromance.info/free-books-and-audiobooks-hot-and-steamy/

Or this one:

https://www.steamyromance.info/the-unexpected-nanny-free/

PREVIEW OF THE BIKER'S GIRL

A Bad Boy and Virgin Romance

by Lily Diamond

~

Blurb

Kitty

When I bought up the large piece of land beside a biker gang's home base, I was only thinking about getting a big enough space to open my animal shelter, Second Chance. Lucky for me the biker gang's full of a harmless bunch of teddy bears—especially when it comes to their dogs. If it weren't for the dogs, I might never have met Jake, the leader of the gang.

I've always had a good relationship with the guys, but I wouldn't mind a little something more from Jake—I haven't been able to stop thinking about him since the moment I met him. But he's never made a move in all this time, and I'm so inexperienced I wouldn't even know where to start on my own.

When an early cold snap threatens autumn litters of kittens throughout the area, I'm left scrambling to distribute insulated nesting shelters and rescue mama cats and their babies all over the area. I need help—and I know just where to get it.

The best part of this plan of mine is that I get to spend the next few weeks riding around from town to town spending time with Jake— who can make my toes curl with just a smile.

∽

Jake

Now and again in my life, I run into a woman so pure and sweet that I just want to get her a little dirty—in all the ways she likes. That's what I think every time I look at sweet, thick little Kitty, who runs the animal shelter next door and keeps my dad's dogs healthy. I would love to make her smile—and scream. I'd even let her leave me with plenty of claw marks. But sweet little Kitty's so shy I'm still trying to figure out how to hit her up without scaring her off.

Now we've got the cutest rescue mission in the damn world on tap for the holidays, and the guys are having as much fun with it as I am. And the more Kitty warms up to me, the closer I get to what I really want for Christmas—her.

CHAPTER ONE

Kitty

It's close to midnight when I make my way up the steps to the Martin farmhouse's pillared, wraparound porch. I'm bundled up against the unseasonable cold; the nights have started dipping below freezing already and it's only November. It worries me—for a lot of reasons. But right now those worries are far from my mind, and I'm trying not to laugh as I approach the door.

I knock on the door and then glance around, smiling. My neighbor down the road has six acres in a long, tree-edged strip that runs back up into the hills. She's a military widow from New York City who decided to retire to the countryside, only to discover that we have our own challenges out here.

Mrs. Annabeth Martin is the kind of sweet old Christian lady who would give you the clothes off her back if she wasn't worried about modesty. She's easily scandalized, tends to pass judgment on people quickly, and is a strange mix of paranoid and naive. I try to be a good neighbor to her, but I always hide the pot and booze before she comes over.

My breath steams past my scarf as I wait for the shuffling footsteps that have started up on the other side of the door. I busy myself by looking around and hoping that I'm wrong about what I suspect I'm going to see when I get inside. The chuckle that sneaks out of me is half ironic.

Annabeth called me apologetically about a friendly stray dog she took in tonight, who turned out to be destructive and not at all housebroken. Since I'm the local vet and run a private animal shelter, I'm the only person in fifty miles that she could turn to. So I only grumbled a little on the way over.

She has two sons who come up from the city on weekends to help look after things, but the land's still looking pretty scruffy. No one has raked the black walnuts off the drive in weeks. The green rinds with their black innards have been torn open by squirrels and left scattered everywhere. The front lawn is adrift with dead leaves.

I turn back to the door as the footsteps get closer and hear the bolt clack as it's thrown. The inner door opens partway, and through the storm door, I see a puffy-haired Annabeth in a fluffy pink robe and big gold cross necklace. She beams as she sees me and hurriedly lets me in. "Come in, dear, come in. He's right in here. Watch your step."

She has spread out newspaper on the floor and I pick my way down the hall as it rustles underfoot. "So where did you find this dog?"

She leads me down her hallway into the kitchen, stopping by the closed door. "Well, he's been coming around begging since the late summer. He doesn't have a collar, so I thought maybe I could win him over and see if he wanted to become my new dog.

"It got so cold tonight that when he cried at the door I let him come running in to warm up, and he seems to want to stay. But he's really a handful. Eats a lot, tries to break into the cabinets, jumps up on the table, pees where he pleases, chews things...it's like he's never lived with a family at all! Not to mention that Mittens is terrified of him."

Oh boy. I am now eighty percent certain about what—and *who*—is hanging out in Annabeth's kitchen. Apparently nobody warned her about one of our neighborhood...characters. "All right, well, let's take a look at him and see what we're dealing with."

The musky smell of something a lot stronger than dog urine hits me as I walk into the kitchen, and I'm careful to watch my step. The culprit, looking fat and very proud of himself, is sitting on the breakfast nook table panting and grinning. I fold my arms and scowl at him, though I can barely keep from laughing.

"Um, Annabeth, sweetie?" I say as the beast on the table squints happily and chuffs at me. "That's...not a dog."

"What do you mean he's not a dog? Isn't he one of those African dogs that don't bark?" She sounds genuinely baffled.

"No, I'm sorry. You see, this is Randy. And he's definitely not a Basenji." I eye Randy as he gives me a saucy look and then starts wagging his tail exactly like a damn dog. No idea where he learned that trick, but it—along with his relative friendliness toward humans—apparently got his paw in the door over here.

"Well, what is he then? He plays, he doesn't bite us, he loves the food we give him..." Poor Annabeth is looking at me like I have sprouted another head.

I sigh. "Annabeth, I'm gonna suggest that you open the back door and let him out. I'm sure he'd be happy to winter with you and have you feed him. And no, he's not gonna bite you, at least not until he's on the couch and you want him to move, or he gets too excited while you're playing."

"But it's so cold! Will he be okay?"

I'm dying here. I'm literally leaving my body as we speak. I shoot a glare at Randy and swear he's laughing at me. "He'll be fine, I promise. He'll catch up with his pack and they'll winter down in the foothills."

My neighbor goes very still. Randy is now licking loudly at his balls. She looks over at him, and hesitantly asks, "Pack...?"

"Randy is a coyote, Annabeth. A spoiled, lazy, sneaky little poop of a coyote who has discovered that if he acts like a cute doggie humans will feed him." I eye Randy up and down, seeing that he's at least five pounds overweight and has a thick, glossy winter pelt. *It's a pretty damn good ploy, actually.*

Randy just grins at me and goes back to licking his balls.

"A coyote?" She stares in amazement. "But he's so friendly!"

"Yeah he is. Humans have food and have a huge soft spot for cute and friendly mammals, and he's figured that out. But look, Annabeth, even if he has discovered humans are easy marks, Randy's a wild animal. He will use your entire house as a toilet, and he will eat your cat."

"Oh no, not Mittens!" She covers her mouth with her hands, eyes wide with horror. I nod gravely, satisfied that she'll think twice before taking in any more "homeless dogs." *Good thing, too, because next time I'll probably come in here to see her new pet has antlers.* Annabeth really is a city girl through and through.

I arch an eyebrow at Randy, who chuffs again and wags his tail. "Forget it, man, nobody here's buying it anymore."

His tail lowers and he yaps at me in irritation, but there's still an edge of smugness to it. *Shithead. Cute, though.*

I'm on my way back to my truck a few minutes later, having calmed my embarrassed neighbor and left her with a bottle of enzyme cleaner. Randy is sitting on the hood of my truck when I reach it, panting and grinning at me. "Fattening up for winter on the old lady's dime, huh? You big mooch."

I can hear the high howls of the other coyotes echoing along the upper slopes. They've caught his scent, and are probably wondering where he was all night. I keep clear of biting range as

I walk around to the driver's side door. "Go on already; go find your pack. They're gonna be pissed you didn't share all your snacks."

He sneezes, then jumps off as I open the door. But instead of running off, his ears prick up suddenly and he looks down the road. I frown and turn on my headlights—just in time to see a feral cat scramble across the road maybe thirty yards away, with a dead rat in her jaws. Her belly hangs loose enough to flap; she's still nursing.

"Damn it." Another late litter. Normally I wouldn't have to worry too much, as local autumn kittens would typically be weaned and have a fighting chance by the time things started freezing over. Not to mention I'd normally have three more weeks to put together the insulated shelters I distribute around the area for the strays every year.

This time, though, there's been no such luck. And as I grab my flashlight and start tracking the feral through the woods, I feel my worry growing.

I'm the shy type. Most of my friends growing up had four legs, and that's still the case now. That's why I got my veterinary degree, why I sunk so much of my inheritance into the private shelter, and why I get pretty upset at the thought of frozen kittens.

I take photos as I go so I can find the cat's nesting spot again once I return with supplies. Finally, I spot the kitty climbing up a dead tree, disappearing into a big hollow about ten feet up. She's picked a good spot. The trunk's thick enough to insulate and protect her babies.

But there are a lot of abandoned and feral cats out here who either won't be as used to the outdoors, or who won't be as lucky in finding a good spot.

Deciding to bring some food and insulating bedding scraps for queen kitty tomorrow, I take a photo of the tree and then turn to go home. *This is a problem that I am going to need some serious help with it. Finding feral litters, sheltering and feeding those we can't relocate to my shelter, distributing the shelter boxes—and doing it all in under a week. Covering miles of road and over a hundred acres.*

My heart sinks. Normally I can get all this done with no problem; my work hours are low even with the shelter to run and the veterinary needs of the valley to take care of. But with my normal workload, the upcoming holidays, the kittens and socialized ex-ferals already in the shelter, and with freezing temperatures arriving three weeks early...

Maybe I can hire some emergency help. It's not like I don't have the cash. People around here don't know that I'm working not because I have to, but because I love what I do. I actually inherited more money than I know what to do with, but I just don't feel right not contributing to my community. Call it my Yankee work ethic.

As I'm driving up the road, I see the coyotes flood across the lane behind me, with Randy's fat butt leading the way. *Nice to see he's back with his family, but they need to go back up their hillside now.* There's another reason to fear for the cats and their kittens —the cold is driving the coyotes downhill too damned soon.

Yeah. I have to fix this.

My house is just up the road. I only drove my truck because it has the big kennel in the back and my dog-catching gear. But I'm not going home yet. I pass the small stone farmhouse and the sprawling barn beyond it, which houses the clinic and shelter. I drive right past my own driveway, headed for my neighbors down the hill on the other side.

The Ravens will still be up. They don't roll up their welcome mat until three. Jake and the guys owe me and I'm sure they wouldn't say no to making some extra cash.

Annabeth would freak out if she knew I was going to the

local biker gang—and resident pot growers—for help. She has this image in her head of what it means to be a biker, and she can't shake the idea that they're all dangerous men, instead of the tough but friendly guys they actually are. But they have never caused me problems, and since I'm the one they go to when their dogs get sick or have puppies, we have a pretty good relationship.

I hope it's good enough. There's an acre-wide strip of trees acting as a buffer between their land and mine, which is home to a lot of wildlife. Beyond it, their high hedges mask their property from the road, but I can see the glow of the house lights through them now that the branches are bare for winter.

My stomach flutters a little as I pull into their gravel driveway and the dusty lot beyond. *I hope Jake is home.*

Big Jake Steele is half the reason I make excuses to come visit. He's the hottest man I have ever seen in my life. Huge, burly—a wild man in leathers with shaggy black hair and a brutally handsome face with intense green eyes. He has a gravelly voice that turns into a slightly awkward purr when he is trying to be less intimidating, and the way his ass looks in his jeans makes it impossible not to stare.

Of course, I've never done a thing about it. But a girl can look...and a girl can dream.

I see his huge shape fill the doorway of the house as I park my truck, and my stomach flutters even harder—but I smile even more.

CHAPTER TWO

Jake

I'm on the couch polishing off my second beer and third coffee when my right-hand man, Morrie, comes in and tells me that Kitty is pulling into the parking lot. A smile breaks over my face; some of my exhaustion lifting off of me like a weight. "I'll go meet her. You guys keep feeding the dogs."

DAD HAS BEEN HAVING a rough night tonight. Nightmares. I took care of him until he felt well enough to want privacy, leaving him with two of the dogs and his bong. But it wore me out, and I was feeling pretty down, right up to the moment I heard Kitty was here.

SOME OF US come back from our time as soldiers with little scars, and some with big ones. Some on them are on the outside for everyone to see, but some, like my dad's, are mostly within. I got my Purple Heart for taking IED shrapnel, and have some scars on my leg and a little limp. My dad never feels safe, and screams himself awake sometimes.

The open road, our club, the pot we grow and smoke, the friends we make on the road and off, and each other—that's what we have to heal us. It works pretty well—that, and Dad's dogs.

I THROW on my jacket on the way out the door, and look out to see Kitty's truck headlights splashed across my front yard. She cuts them off and gets out, then heads for me, waving. I grin and raise a hand. "Evening!"

"HI THERE!" she calls up, and I try to fight my smile down, but the sight of her warms me. She's small, sweet-faced and very curvy, with a dynamite rack that even layers of clothing can't hide. She's got fluffy, curly hair the color of honey, eyes nearly the exact same shade, and a smile that's contagious.

IT'S PRETTY rare for me to meet someone that I want to hang out with all the time, cuddle silly, and fuck unconscious, all at the same time. Usually I just want to do one or two of the three when I meet a lady, but Kitty is special.

TOO BAD THAT if I proposed the sex part, I'd probably scare her off. She's sweet, shy, and tiny. I'm roughly the size of a truck, hung to match, and keep company with ex-convicts. I know she knows I would never hurt her, but the logistics alone would take some work to overcome.

I HATE BEING STUCK JUST WATCHING and wanting, but the fact that she's an awesome friend eases that frustration a bit. She gets along with everyone, we trade favors all the time, and my Dad loves her because she takes care of his dogs for him. But lately, I can't even finish with a woman unless I'm thinking about Kitty.

SHE SMILES UP AT ME, and it warms me on this cold night, even as I stand in front of her with my jacket open. "Hey, do you have a few minutes, or is this a bad time?"

"NO WORRIES, sweetheart. C'mon up, I've got a beer with your name on it." I step back, holding the door open for her as she bounces up the stairs. Immediately, happy barking starts up in the back of the house, and the whole pack scrambles toward the door at once. They know her and love her.

SOME WOMEN BECOME crazy cat ladies. My Dad calls himself a crazy dog guy. We laugh over it. But these rescue dogs—mostly pit bulls we saved from a fighting ring—give Dad a reason to get out of bed when he's having a rough time.

I DO whatever it takes to help him. The crash that disabled him and left me in charge of the bike club also made his PTSD worse. So, early last year, when he told me being around dogs helped his mood, we went looking for a puppy for him.

. . .

Now the compound has seven. Four brindle and white Pits, a Rottie, a Husky-Tibetan mastiff mix named Chewbacca, and Laughing Boy, a coyote-dog hybrid whose dad, Randy, keeps visiting the neighborhood. They crowd around us, their tails wagging uncontrollably, as I lead Kitty inside.

"Hi boys! Hi Maggie!" Her voice is bright as they press in to get their hugs. I kind of wish I could line up with them and get a hug too.

It really is a bunch of guys in this household; even the dogs. The whole crew is a sausage fest except for Maggie Grue, the oldest pit bull and mother to the others. Just sorta worked out that way.

Kitty disappears halfway into Chewbacca's russet fur as she hugs him, and he pants happily. *Goddamn, she's adorable.* And her nice, round ass looks great in those jeans, too.

Like me, she likes to wind down with a coffee and a beer in each hand on cold nights. I pour her a mug and pull a longneck out of the fridge, and then come back into the living room to find her on one of the big, blanket-covered couches that line the room. Chewie has his head in her lap and she's already got a grooming brush in her hand.

. . .

"So, what can I do for you, sweetheart?" I ask as I flop onto the couch kitty-corner to hers. Two of the pits, Bo and Maggie, hop onto the couch next to me, and the others settle around our feet.

"I need your help—you and the guys. You know cold season has come early. That's big trouble for the local feral cats, and I have to prepare for winter three weeks early—and as fast as possible." Her face is serious as she works on the endless task of combing out Chewie's fur.

"Yeah, I noticed the coyotes are passing through the neighborhood early. The cold's driving all their prey downhill." I frown as I set her drinks on the coffee table in front of her and set the bottle of chocolate syrup within reach. "You seen Randy around?"

She snorts and reaches for the coffee first, setting aside the brush for a bit. She squirts syrup into her mug and stirs it as she talks. "Yeah. He's fine. He conned Annabeth into thinking he was a stray dog. She's been feeding him on her porch for weeks on top of his hunting with his pack. He looks like a sausage in a fur coat now."

I let out a bark of laughter, imagining it. That damn coyote is hilarious, but he's also a menace. If he can't eat your pet or livestock then he tries to eat their food, and when he's done with their food he tries to mate with them.

. . .

THE RESULT IS a local coydog problem that gave the little fucker his name, and led to Kitty offering free spay-neuter procedures for local pets. Laffy, who knows the word "Randy," keeps pricking up his ears as we talk. He was part of a half-German Shepherd litter of six.

KITTY TAKES an experimental sip of her makeshift mocha, and then a larger swallow. "The last few years, even with the spay and release program for the feral cats, we've had at least ten litters every autumn in the woods around here. A few of the queens will be smart in their choice of nests and will just need some help with food, but some will need to be completely relocated."

I NOD, frowning a little. It's a busy time for us; we've just got the autumn pot crop in and the whole thing is drying under the greenhouse tents. But I know I can't say no to her. Besides, if enough of the boys help out, we can handle the whole mess in a few days.

AND AFTER THAT she'll need help socializing kittens, which is hardly work at all.

"TEN LITTERS. And you've got room for them?" I lift an eyebrow. I don't know how she gets as much done in that shelter as she does—she must have either a pile of money I don't know about, or some kind of magic. She has a website, volunteers, people doing adoption days for her in cities and towns up and down the coast...and she just expanded her facilities again last year.

. . .

"Oh yeah, unless it's like ten litters of twelve or something. Then I might have a problem." She gives a little nervous laugh. Chewie whines at her, desperate to regain her attention, and she goes back to brushing him.

"I know I can get some of the guys to help out. We have to have at least four of us dealing with the curing process, but that leaves six guys to help you out."

"Seven," I heard my Dad's voice in the doorway, sounding tired but determined.

We look up to see him walking in with his cane, his grizzled face looking calm but focused. Dad and I resemble each other so closely that I pretty much know what I'm going to look like in about twenty-five years. Little grayer, little jowlier. Only the cane gives him any real appearance of being old.

"So what's going on?" he asks, limping over and plopping into his overstuffed chair across from the couch I'm perched on. He has his bong in his grip, and loads it from an Altoids tin while he listens to her explanation.

"Kitten season," she starts, and goes back over what she told me. He nods along, then takes a long hit and holds it before passing her the bong. She hesitates before taking a hit. "Annabeth would be shocked to see me smoking like this."

"Annabeth shocks too easily. This would help her plenty with her arthritis, and besides, it's been legal for years now," I say, noticing Dad shoot me a look to tell me to shut up about the old church lady. He's got a soft spot in his head for war widows, and it's not like Annabeth isn't a nice person.

But the truth is she's called the police on us twenty times in just the last year, and all for bullshit reasons. Guns we don't own, drugs we don't run, "suspicious people," noise complaints about our motorcycles in the middle of the afternoon. The cops are sick of her, but they can't really explain to their boss why the local (wealthy) innocent war widow keeps calling in a panic if nothing is going on.

"She does shock too easily, and she prejudges people. But I can manage her. I'll just get permission to search her acres myself. She owes me a favor now." She shoots my dad a placating look, and he nods with a faint smile.

"Anyway, point is, you'll have plenty of help," I'm confident in promising. "When will you need us?"

She flashes me that heart-warming smile again, eyes full of relief. "Mid-afternoon tomorrow would be great, or the next day if you have trouble pulling things together on time."

. . .

I NOD and revel in that smile, and in how she's looking at me. It makes a guy a little too hopeful. But I'll manage. I always do. "We'll be there tomorrow. No sweat. Now how about you pass me that bong and we'll make plans."

If you want to continue reading this story, you can get your copy from your favorite vendor by searching for the title:

The Biker's Girl

A Bad Boy and Virgin Romance

You can also find the e-book version by typing this link in your computer's browser:

https://www.hotandsteamyromance.com/products/the-biker-s-girl-a-bad-boy-a-virgin-romance

OTHER BOOKS BY THIS AUTHOR

Saving Her Rescuer: A Billionaire & A Virgin Romance

I was just trying to get away from my crazy ex for the weekend when I ended up in a giant pileup on the highway up to Gore Mountain.

https://geni.us/SavingHerRescuer

~

Sensual Sounds: A Rockstar Ménage

Lust. Lies. Double lives.

The rock and roll industry is full of people who are looking out for themselves and willing to do anything to rise to the top.

https://www.hotandsteamyromance.com/collections/frontpage/products/sensual-sounds-a-rockstar-menage

~

On the Run: A Secret Baby Romance

Murder. Lies. Fraud. Just another day in the lives of billionaires and women on the run.

https://www.hotandsteamyromance.com/collections/frontpage/products/on-the-run-a-secret-baby-romance

~

The Dirty Doctor's Touch: A Billionaire Doctor Romance

I am a master. An elitist. I am at the top of my field, and I know what I am doing.

https://www.hotandsteamyromance.com/collections/frontpage/products/the-dirty-doctor-s-touch-a-billionaire-doctor-romance

The Hero She Needs: A Single Daddy Next Door Romance

He's the only man I've ever wanted...

https://www.hotandsteamyromance.com/collections/frontpage/products/the-hero-she-needs-a-single-daddy-next-door-romance

You can find all of my books here:

Hot and Steamy Romance

https://www.hotandsteamyromance.com

Facebook

facebook.com/HotAndSteamyRomance

COPYRIGHT

©Copyright 2020 by Alisha Star- All rights Reserved
In no way is it legal to reproduce, duplicate, or transmit any part of this document in either electronic means or in printed format. Recording of this publication is strictly prohibited and any storage of this document is not allowed unless with written permission from the publisher. All rights are reserved. Respective authors own all copyrights not held by the publisher.

www.ingramcontent.com/pod-product-compliance
Lightning Source LLC
LaVergne TN
LVHW011709060526
838200LV00051B/2823